Halfway up the third set of stai
fire door slamming open again:
stairwell. A split second later a bloodcurdling scream echoed
above me. I looked up to find a billowing mass of tie-dyed
rainbow chiffon plummeting toward me. As I flattened myself
against the wall, Lovinia Darling's body landed with a bone-
shattering thud at my feet.

Praise for *Definitely Dead*
An Empty Nest Mystery, Book One

Books by Lois Winston

Anastasia Pollack Crafting Mystery series
Assault with a Deadly Glue Gun
Death by Killer Mop Doll
Revenge of the Crafty Corpse
Decoupage Can Be Deadly
A Stitch to Die For
Scrapbook of Murder
Drop Dead Ornaments
Handmade Ho-Ho Homicide
A Sew Deadly Cruise
Stitch, Bake, Die!
Guilty as Framed

Anastasia Pollack Crafting Mini-Mysteries
Crewel Intentions
Mosaic Mayhem
Patchwork Peril
Crafty Crimes (all 3 novellas in one volume)

Empty Nest Mystery Series
Definitely Dead
Literally Dead

Romantic Suspense
Love, Lies and a Double Shot of Deception
Lost in Manhattan (writing as Emma Carlyle)
Someone to Watch Over Me (writing as Emma Carlyle)

Romance and Chick Lit
Talk Gertie to Me
Four Uncles and a Wedding (writing as Emma Carlyle)
Hooking Mr. Right (writing as Emma Carlyle)
Finding Hope (Writing as Emma Carlyle)

Novellas and Novelettes
Elementary, My Dear Gertie
Moms in Black, A Mom Squad Caper
Once Upon a Romance
Finding Mr. Right

Children's Chapter Book
The Magic Paintbrush

Nonfiction
Top Ten Reasons Your Novel is Rejected
House Unauthorized
Bake, Love, Write
We'd Rather Be Writing

Literally
Dead

LOIS WINSTON

Cover design by L. Winston

ISBN-9781940795386

ACKNOWLEDGMENTS

Enormous thanks to Donnell Bell and Irene Peterson for their critiquing and editing skills.

ONE

The wheels of my suitcase couldn't spin fast enough as I pushed through the revolving door of the Crown Jewel Hotel in midtown Manhattan. Once inside the lobby, I stopped short and gazed awestruck, soaking in the writerly atmosphere. My heart pounded so fast I could hear it reverberating in my ears. Or maybe that was the din of the voices from hundreds of romance authors filling the forty-story marble and glass atrium.

My eyes bugged out as I scoped the room. "Oh my God, Blake!" I reached for my husband's hand and squeezed it. "That's Liz Phillips," I released my grip on my suitcase handle and pointed in the direction of the bar off to my right. "And Elise Robertson."

"Friends of yours?" asked my husband.

"I wish! They're two of the most successful romance writers in the world. I can't believe I'm standing only a few yards away from them!" Talk about a fan girl moment! One more superstar sighting and I just might need a brown paper bag to ward off imminent hyperventilation.

"Hurry!" I pulled him along, nearly tripping over my Kate Spades as I race-walked toward the shortest of several lines that serpentined from the hotel registration desk around the chic silver, white, and gray lobby.

Blake grabbed me, preventing me from executing a face plant. Then he spun me around and settled his hands on my shoulders. Lowering his head until our foreheads nearly touched, he said, "I know you're excited, Gracie, but take a deep breath. Slow down. The conference doesn't start for several hours. You're not going to miss anything."

I humored him by continuing at a jog instead of a sprint until I reached the back of the line. "I can't believe I'm here!" I squealed, bouncing on the balls of my feet.

A year of slaving over my manuscript had finally paid off. "Just think, by this time next year I'll probably be returning as Gracie Elliott, published romance author."

"Don't you mean Emma Carlyle?"

"Right. Sorry." Since Blake didn't think the stuffy old academics of the university governing board would take too kindly to a faculty wife writing sensuous romances—not that my writing rose anywhere near *Fifty Shades* level—I'd promised to publish under a pseudonym. Thus, Gracie Elliott would become Emma Carlyle on bookstore shelves.

"Besides, aren't you forgetting something?"

"Like what?"

"You need to sell your book first."

Leave it to Mr. Logical to burst my bubble. "Yes, of course, but I'm sure I'll have plenty of offers here at the conference. After all, I'm the winner of the Society of American Romance Author's Cream of the Crop writing competition. That's a huge award. You should be excited for me, Blake. And proud of my accomplishment."

"I am excited for you, sweetheart, and I've always been proud of you. You're the most amazing woman I've ever met. You set yourself a goal, and you work until you accomplish it." He pecked my cheek. "I just don't want to see you disappointed."

"Why would I be disappointed? You just said I always accomplish my goals, didn't you?"

"Yes, but some goals take longer than others. Did winning this contest guarantee you a publishing contract?"

"No, but—"

"The win gives you the opportunity to attend this writing conference, nothing more. Let's keep everything in perspective, okay?"

"Fine. But you're going to eat those practical words of yours by the end of these three days."

"I'd love nothing better than to see you prove me wrong."

We inched our way up in line. "Notice anything odd?" he asked above the cacophony of conversations around us.

I glanced up at my husband, then around the massive lobby. "Odd?" Although this was my first writing conference, I'd attended my share of business conferences and conventions over the years. Prior to the industry downsizing that outsourced my job as a fabric designer overseas and left me jobless and pension-less, I'd spent many hours cooling my Kate Spades and Christian Louboutins in long, slow-moving hotel check-in lines. "Not really."

"It's a veritable estrogen brigade here, Gracie!" My normally unflappable husband suddenly looked like the clueless hero of a fish-out-of-water romance novel.

I did notice several women eyeing Blake. Nothing new there. Heads always turn when we enter a room, but never in my direction. Women always zero in on Blake, especially widows, divorcees, and campus coeds. With the exception of his shock of silver hair, my middle-aged husband could pass for Hugh Jackman. I needed Wolverine claws to fend off some of the more aggressive ones. "Most of them probably think you're an agent or a publisher," I said. *And that I'm your assistant*, I added to myself.

Not that I have low self-esteem. I'm simply bowing to the obvious. I'm not bad looking, just your average middle-aged woman—average height, average figure, average brown hair. My one outstanding feature is that I have one green eye and one blue eye, like Gracie Allen, which is what first caught Blake's attention. He was researching early nineteen-fifties television at the time, and I reminded him of the late comedienne in both looks and mannerisms. Except Gracie Allen was acting. My sometimes harebrained, scatterbrained nature is ingrained in my DNA.

Blake, on the other hand, is so far above average, he resides on another planet in a galaxy far, far away—an invitation-only planet reserved strictly for celebrities and guys who resemble celebrities.

My husband speared me with *The Look*, the expression he reserves for those times when I ramble to the tune of my own off-key, off-kilter symphony. "Are you sure we're at the right hotel? This looks more like a Mary Kay convention than a writing conference. Where are all the men?"

"I see men." I motioned around the lobby. "Two reservation clerks behind the desk, one at the concierge station, three bellhops—"

"You know what I mean. *Male* authors."

I rolled my eyes. My husband might be brilliant when it comes to his own field of expertise—twentieth century culture and counter-culture and its influences on the media—but he obviously knew nothing about twenty-first century romance fiction, a field dominated by women. I shrugged. "At the thriller writers and sci-fi writers conferences?"

"She's right," said someone behind us. "Very few men write romance."

Blake and I turned to face the woman who belonged to the voice and who had obviously been eavesdropping on our conversation. She sported a chestnut pixie haircut streaked with silver and a smattering of fine laugh lines at the corners of her eyes and mouth.

OMG! I recognized her immediately. A third romance superstar, and this one was standing right behind me and speaking to us! My jaw flapped open and closed several times before words spilled out. Finally I said, "You're Paisley Prentiss!"

She held her hand out to me. "Guilty."

I grabbed her hand in both of mine and gave it an enthusiastic shake. "I'm a huge fan! I've read all your books."

"Thank you. And you are?"

"Gracie Elliott."

She smiled, her laugh lines deepening as she extricated her hand. "First-timer?"

Did I have a bright red neon *Romance Writer Wannabe* sign flashing above my head? "Is it that obvious?"

She cocked her head toward Blake. "Husband?"

I nodded. "Blake Elliott."

Paisley chuckled. "Dead giveaway. Most of us leave our spouses at home. They tend to get in the way of our fun."

Blake shot me *The Look*.

"I wanted him here to see me accept the Cream of the Crop Award," I said.

"Congratulations. I remember my first contest win. It was very exciting."

"Did you sell your book as a result of winning a contest?" asked Blake.

"Heavens, no! Writing contests are a way for writers to gain feedback and hone their skills. They rarely result in anything beyond that."

"Really?" My heart plummeted to my toes. "But won't I meet agents and editors here? Shouldn't they want to read my book?"

"Some might, but don't give up hope if no one does."

"But—"

She placed her hand on my upper arm. "It's a process, Gracie, usually a very long process. I wrote for ten years before I sold my first book."

"You? But you're Paisley Prentiss. Your romantic comedies are a constant fixture on the *New York Times* bestseller list."

"And once upon a time I stood here just like you—wide-eyed and hopeful—until the reality of the publishing industry smacked me upside the head. Rejection happens. A lot. Even to published authors. Those who eventually succeed do so because they don't give up. The trick is to keep writing. Keep learning. Keep submitting your work. If you're lucky, someday your efforts will pay off, and you'll sell your first book."

Someday? I don't have *someday*. I'm forty-seven years old and unemployed with two kids in college and a husband whose professor salary doesn't begin to allow us to think about a comfortable retirement, let alone pay for my designer shoes and handbag addiction.

To his credit Blake refrained from saying, "I told you so," but I knew he was thinking it. Instead, he wrapped his arm around my shoulders and changed the subject. "So, Paisley, you say there are no male romance writers? What about all those sappy tearjerkers I've seen in bookstores over the years?"

"Which ones?"

Blake thought for a moment. "There's that one about the covered bridges in Iowa. And the one where it turns out the wife has dementia. Weren't they written by men?"

"Yes, but those books aren't romances."

Blake scoffed. "Of course they are."

Paisley shook her head and held up a finger. "First rule of romance: the story *must* have an HEA."

"HEA?"

"Happily ever after," I informed my husband.

"Those guys don't write HEA," explained Paisley. "Someone always winds up leaving or dying. Or leaving, then dying."

Blake wasn't buying it. "So you're saying *Romeo and Juliet* isn't a love story? I believe every Shakespearean scholar in the world would disagree with you."

"Love story, yes. Romance, no."

Blake shrugged. "Semantics."

"No, there's a big difference. At least in the publishing world."

I yanked on Blake's sleeve. "Stop arguing. This is Paisley Prentiss. She knows what she's talking about."

"There are a few male romance authors," Paisley continued. "Some write in partnership with their wives; others write on their own. But they all write under pen names."

She pointed to a grouping of chairs a few feet from where we stood and whispered, "See that dumpy old guy in the baggy jeans,

7

suspenders, plaid shirt, and cowboy hat? He's written over a hundred historical romances as Penelope McGregor."

"*He's* Penelope McGregor?" I asked way too loudly. Several heads turned in my direction—including Penelope McGregor's. *Whoops!* He skewered me with a killer scowl as he used a cane to heave his massive body out of the chair. I quickly looked away, but it was too late. The intense heat of embarrassment suffusing my face pegged me as the blurting culprit.

"Hard to believe, isn't it?" asked Paisley as Penelope McGregor turned her—his—back on us and with great difficulty lumbered toward the bank of elevators.

"I'll say," I muttered. Given the level of steam in her—his—books, I expected Penelope McGregor to look more like the late Barbara Cartland than an eighty-year-old version of *Southpark's* Eric Cartman.

"He keeps his real name a closely guarded secret," said Paisley. "Rumor has it he holds some highly sensitive government position and would lose his job if his bosses ever connected him to Penelope."

"He'd have to present ID to check into the hotel," said my ever-logical husband.

Paisley shrugged. "I suppose he's got some way of working around that. Besides, the hotel would never divulge personal information about a guest to anyone."

"Unless TMZ paid off a desk clerk," said Blake.

Paisley considered that for a moment. "I don't think TMZ is interested in romance authors. We're not high enough up on the celebrity food chain for them."

Through my partially obstructed view, I continued to stare at Penelope McGregor's back as he waited for an elevator. When the doors of the elevator directly in front of him opened, an extremely tall, overly Rubenesque woman exited, nearly barreling into him. When he refused to budge, instead of stepping around him, she stiff-armed him out of her way.

Penelope McGregor lost his balance and teetered backwards, his cowboy hat flying off his head. Several people behind him reached out and grabbed hold of his arms, preventing him from landing on his rump. Without so much as a glance in his direction, the woman who had pushed him stormed toward the registration desk.

"Here comes trouble," said Paisley.

"Isn't that Lovinia Darling?" I asked. Even though I hadn't gotten a good look at her face, I recognized the trademark vintage Pucci attire and platinum beehive hairdo of the most famous of all living romance authors.

"The devil herself."

The crowds had thinned as people crowded into several elevators. I watched as a younger woman who had followed behind Lovinia placed her hand on Penelope McGregor's forearm and said something to him.

Although I couldn't hear what she said, he answered her in a booming voice that filled the lobby. "You should be ashamed of yourself, always making excuses for that woman."

Heads turned in their direction. A hush settled across the lobby, making her reply audible to those of us standing nearby. "I didn't mean—"

He jerked his arm from her grasp. "Save it. I know what you meant." He turned and having missed his chance to enter the first elevator, headed toward another currently discharging passengers.

She stared at his retreating back as he stepped inside and the doors closed behind him. Then she scurried off to catch up with Lovinia.

By this point Lovinia Darling had pushed her way to the front of the registration line to our right, elbowing aside a woman in the process of checking in. We had progressed far enough along our own line that I had a clear view of Lovinia's back.

The woman she'd pushed aside opened her mouth to object but took one look at the rude buttinsky, snapped her mouth shut, and stepped aside. You'd think the Queen of England had just cut in line in front of her.

Lovinia Darling smacked her key card onto the counter and in a voice that carried across the lobby asked, "Do you know what this is?"

The reservation clerk glanced at the plastic. "Your room key, ma'am."

"*Room* being the operative word here."

With condescension dripping from his voice, he asked, "Is there a problem?"

"There most certainly is a problem. I'm supposed to have a deluxe suite, not a *room*." She turned to the woman who had followed after her. "Don't just stand there like a lizard napping on a rock. Show this pompous *clerk* the paperwork."

The woman reached into an enormous leather satchel and withdrew a folder crammed with papers. She began thumbing through sheets while Lovinia Darling stood, hands on hips, impatiently tapping what I recognized as a fifteen hundred dollar pair of Jimmy Choo anthracite glitter Lorelai pumps. "It's here somewhere," said the woman, her voice quivering. "I know it is."

"I don't know why she puts up with such abuse," said Paisley.

"Who is she?"

"Marcella Ford, Lovinia's personal assistant."

"Oh, for the love of—!" Lovinia snatched the papers from Marcella's hand. "What good are you? Must I do everything myself?"

Marcella cowered from Lovinia's verbal assault, visibly shrinking into herself as the scene unfolded before us. The petite woman was no match for her larger-than-life bully employer.

I made a mental note to strike Lovinia Darling from my automatic buy list. No way would she ever see a dime of royalties from me ever again, no matter how much I'd previously enjoyed her books.

Lovinia quickly rifled through the papers, pulled one from the pile, and slammed it onto the counter. "Here!" She pointed to something on the page. "Right there it states a deluxe suite. Not a *room*. *I* don't do *rooms*."

By now all the other women waiting in line had ceased their chatter, their eyes directed toward the drama playing out at the front desk.

The clerk perused the paper, typed something on his keyboard, then consulted his computer terminal. "Your paperwork is from the conference, ma'am. The conference may have promised you a suite, but they only paid for a room for you. One room with two queen beds for two occupants." He pushed the paper back toward her. "If there's been a mistake, it's on the part of the conference. You'll have to take this up with them. Now please step aside. You're holding up the line."

Lovinia threw back her shoulders and appeared to grow several inches taller than her already six-foot frame. "Young man, do you have any idea who I am?"

"No, ma'am, and I really don't care."

She fisted the counter. "I demand to speak with the hotel manager."

"I *am* the hotel manager, and I'll be happy to upgrade you to a suite if either you or the conference pays for it. Barring that, you'll have to be satisfied with your *room*."

Lovinia Darling spun around and began berating her assistant. "This is your fault, Marcella."

"How...I—" She snuffled and blinked furiously behind thick black frame glasses, but even from my vantage point of several feet away I could see she failed miserably. Her entire body trembled as tears streamed down her cheeks.

"Oh, stop blubbering!" Lovinia waved her hand in dismissal. "Go find the conference chair and straighten out this mess. I'll be in the bar." She turned on her Lorelais, threw back her shoulders, and with head held high, strutted across the lobby.

Blake had remained uncharacteristically silent during *As the Romance World Turns* played out before us. Now, as the chatter in the lobby resumed at an even higher decibel level than the pre-Lovinia Darling episode, he turned to me and said, "Sure you wouldn't rather write cozy mysteries, Gracie? Or better yet, how about children's books?"

I'd considered mystery, especially after discovering Sidney Mandelbaum stabbed to death in the parking lot of the Moose Lodge. Sid had been one of my clients earlier in the year, during my brief foray as a wing woman for the senior set. I'd even discovered his killer, although it nearly cost me my life.

My heart belonged to romance, though. Just because the most famous romance writer in the world turned out to be more like Cruella de Vil than the sweet small town heroines she created, I saw no reason to switch genres. "I'm sure there are plenty of prima donnas in the worlds of mystery and kid lit," I said. Pausing a beat, I added, "Just as there are in academia."

Blake responded with *The Look*. I ignored him, not because I didn't have a pithy retort on the tip of my tongue but because we'd finally reached the front of the registration line.

I gave my name to the desk clerk and held my breath. As part of the contest win, the conference had comped my room. After the drama surrounding Lovinia Darling, I worried that they might not have conveyed this information to the hotel. Blake would have a cow if we had to shell out more than seven hundred dollars for two nights at the Crown Jewel Hotel, especially since we live less than twenty miles away and I could easily commute into Manhattan for the three-day conference.

However, I needn't have worried. The clerk only requested ID and a credit card to keep on file for incidentals since the conference wasn't picking up the tab for pay-per-view or mini-bar charges. Not that I'd have time to watch a movie or would ever consider helping myself to a five-dollar granola bar.

Before heading to our room, I turned one last time to Paisley. "I'm so glad I had a chance to meet you. Maybe we'll bump into each other at a workshop."

"I have a better idea," she said. "I'm in charge of setting up for the banquet tonight. Why don't you join us? I can always use another volunteer, and it will give you a chance to meet some of the other authors."

Really? I couldn't believe my ears. Paisley Prentiss wanted me to hang out with her and her fellow authors? Had I just died and gone to publishing heaven? Trying my hardest to sound like a professional writer and not some teenybopper at a One Direction concert, I said, "I'd love to. Thank you so much."

"Great. We're meeting in the dining room at four-thirty." She executed a quick eye-sweep of my classic Ann Taylor black linen business suit and gray silk blouse, one of my wardrobe staples for attending business events. Her scrutiny puzzled me. Paisley wore an outfit more suited to a quick trip to the supermarket. I stole a glance at the other women around me. That's when I realized, except for the Pucci-clad Lovinia Darling, nearly every other woman in the lobby was dressed in jeans or khakis.

"Wear jeans and sneakers," said Paisley.

"I thought the banquet was formal." My business experience had taught me that a woman, especially one in a male-dominated profession, needed to present herself in a professional manner at all times. Romance writers might wear pajamas and bunny slippers as they sat at home in front of their computers, but this was a conference where publishers, editors, and agents would be in attendance. Shouldn't everyone dress appropriately?

Or perhaps, since the conference didn't officially begin until the banquet this evening, they didn't feel the need for business attire this afternoon. Still, you never knew whom you might meet in a hotel lobby. First impressions were often lasting impressions, and my twenty-five years of experience in the textile industry had taught me it's always best to make a good first impression.

"Yes, tonight is formal," said Paisley, "but we'll be hauling cartons of books."

When I frowned, she patted me on the arm and added, "Don't worry. You'll have plenty of time to change your clothes before dinner."

"Okay. Four-thirty. See you there."

Before heading up to our room, Blake and I made a quick detour up the escalator to the mezzanine level where the SARA conference registration was taking place. I gave my name to the woman behind the registration table.

"Our Cream of the Crop winner? Congratulations!" She handed me a large canvas tote stuffed with books and an envelope containing my conference badge and seat assignment for the banquet. A pink ribbon with gold lettering that read *First Place Cream of the Crop* hung from beneath the badge. I couldn't take my eyes off it as Blake and I walked toward the elevator.

"If your grin gets any wider," he said, "your cheeks will crack."

But the pride I saw in his eyes made me want to break out in a combination Whip/Nae Nae/Snoopy dance. Only the knowledge of my own innate clumsiness—not to mention the certainty of my three-inch Kate Spade heels sliding out from under me on the marble floor—held me back. I'd already nearly executed a scene from a slapstick comedy when I first entered the hotel. Why tempt fate a second time? Blake did have a point, though. I probably looked totally goofy.

As if reading my mind, he wrapped his arm around my shoulders and drew me close. We then squeezed into an elevator car that immediately went from crowded to over-crowded with the addition of two more riders, our wheeled luggage, and the book-laden conference tote bag dangling from my arm. "Enjoy the moment, Gracie," Blake whispered in my ear as we scrunched together like sardines in a tin. "You've earned it."

Some men are embarrassed by what their romance author wives write. If Blake harbored any misgivings about my new career, he never once mentioned them—other than to request I use a pen name—and that stemmed from not wanting to jeopardize his job security. With only one of us now holding a full-time position, I completely understood his request.

Besides, thanks to the free-flowing booze at most faculty functions, too many professors regularly make complete fools of themselves. If Blake's colleagues learned I write romance, we'd both continually have to fend off boorish questions and comments pertaining to how I researched my sex scenes. A pen name spared us both from having to deal with that.

As the doors began to close in front of me, Lovinia Darling shouted, "Hold that elevator!" as she strode the last few feet toward us.

The woman behind me muttered, "Not if my life depended on it."

I guess she wasn't a member of the Lovinia Darling fan club, but even if the car had been filled with Darling devotees, this sardine can had already reached capacity. Thankfully, with Blake and me being the last two people to enter the car, a certain part of his anatomy wasn't pressing against the backside of a woman who wasn't his wife. However, the two women standing behind us were way too close for comfort. I'm not keen on having a stranger's tatas up close and personal with any part of my husband. With not a millimeter of space between bodies, we certainly had no room for anyone else, let alone a woman in need of a Weight Watchers membership.

No one near the control panel made any effort to jab the button to hold the door open, not that they could have moved had they wanted to accommodate Lovinia. As the doors closed in her face, Lovinia Darling pursed her lips and shot me a stink eye.

"Do you think there's any truth to that rumor?" asked another woman standing somewhere behind me.

"Could be. It's not the first accusation," said the not-if-my-life-depended-on-it woman.

"Really?"

"The first one that I know of happened at least twenty-five years ago. Nothing ever came of it. I've heard rumors of others over the years, but I have no idea if they're true or not. Anyway, plagiarism is hard to prove."

Plagiarism? Were they talking about Lovinia Darling? *Holy guacamole!*

"Not any more," chimed in a third woman. Back then we didn't have ebooks, social media, and advanced search engines. Nowadays it's much easier to unmask a plagiarist."

Blake and I exchanged a knowing look. At the start of every school year he caught freshman turning in assignments they'd blatantly copied from the Internet. Some of the papers were even ones Blake himself had published! Often the plagiarist didn't even bother to check the author's name before copying the essay and pasting it into a new Word document with his own name.

"True," said the not-if-my-life-depended-on-it woman. "Sometimes all it takes is one observant fan to alert you to similarities in books. A bit of digging does the rest. Makes you wonder, doesn't it?"

"About what?" the second woman asked.

"How long she's been doing it," said the third woman. "Possibly years. And she wouldn't be the first. Remember what happened to Jeanette Weeks? She not only stole storylines, she lifted entire passages from various authors' books and cobbled them together."

"I forgot about that," said the second woman. "Didn't she blame the stress of a failing marriage?"

Not-if-my-life-depended-on-it snorted.

Just then the elevator came to a halt at our floor. Blake and I stepped out. As the doors swooshed closed behind us, he turned to me and raised an eyebrow. "Rethinking your career as a romance author yet, Gracie?"

"Why?"

"This writing organization is a den of iniquity."

"Every profession has its bad apples."

"I'm still waiting to find a few good ones here," said Blake.

"What about Paisley? She seems perfectly nice."

"As long as she's not the plagiarist."

"Really, Blake! Besides, I believe the women in the elevator were referring to Lovinia Darling."

"Time will tell."

TWO

Blake and I entered our hotel room to find ourselves immediately transported back to the nineteen-seventies. Bulky faux walnut Mediterranean furniture filled the room. Headache-inducing op art in varying shades of brown, green, and orange papered all four walls. The quilted bedspread was a striped orange, gold, and avocado polyester monstrosity. Even the television, a massive tube-style, harkened back at least forty years. The room looked like a set straight out of a mid-century sit-com. Blake should feel right at home.

Not me. I wrinkled my nose at the carpet, wondering how many germs lurked within the multi-colored gold and brown shag strands. No way was I walking barefoot on that! "Looks like they used up their decorating budget on the lobby," I said.

"I think I read somewhere that they're in the process of a major renovation," said Blake. "I guess they haven't gotten to all the guest rooms yet."

"I suppose I have no right to complain, given that we're not paying for the room."

"We could take the train home after the banquet tonight."

Tempting as that sounded, I didn't want to miss a minute of the conference by having to waste time commuting back and forth over the weekend. I'd heard that a writer could learn as much or more by hanging out in the lobby and the bar than from attending the workshops at writing conferences.

I glanced around at the room, then stuck my head into the bathroom for a quick inspection. The gold Formica countertop contained a few chips and cigarette burns from back when the hotel allowed smoking, but I saw no evidence of mold, or mildew in the tub/shower combo. Still, a little elbow grease would certainly go a long way. "I suppose I can tough it out for two nights if you can."

"Your decision," said Blake. "You're the neat freak. I'm the one who took the kids camping in the woods while you stayed home."

I returned to my husband and planted a quick kiss on his lips. "And for that I will always be eternally grateful." Vacations should be all about luxury and relaxation, not having more work and being more uncomfortable than I am in my bug-free, climate-controlled home.

~*~

After unpacking, I changed into a pair of jeans and my red scoop neck "I'm in my *write* mind" T-shirt. Leaving Blake to grade his students' final exams, I headed downstairs to the ballroom to help Paisley and the other volunteers.

With its mirrored walls and massive rows of crystal chandeliers, the cavernous Crown Jewel Hotel ballroom mimicked the Hall of Mirrors at Versailles. The effect struck me as rather incongruous with the minimalist décor of the lobby and suggested either dueling decorators or one totally screwball designer experimenting with odd style mash-ups.

Or perhaps the ballroom hadn't undergone its scheduled update yet. The sounds of hammering and power tools filtered down from the floor above. Blake must be right about the hotel still being in the throes of renovations.

I estimated roughly a hundred large round tables filling the room, each table surrounded by ten gold painted chairs with white cushions and gold piping. Enormous pink linen bows were tied to the seatbacks. The catering staff had already dressed the tables in pink linen with gold chargers, gold-banded white china, gold-plated cutlery, and gold-rimmed crystal goblets. A pink napkin folded to resemble a Bird of Paradise adorned the center of each dinner plate. A massive arrangement of pink hydrangeas filled the center of each table. A gold cardholder rose from the middle of each centerpiece, the white place cards designating either table numbers or specific board members or chairpersons.

I'd attended dozens of business conferences and dinners throughout my career in the textile industry, and I knew this amount of elegance wasn't standard hotel set-up for such events. To minimize costs most organizations opt for a basic package, along with the standard "conference chicken" entrée. The Society of American Romance Authors had definitely paid big bucks for a premier banquet package with the ballroom decked out more for an upscale wedding than a writing conference.

Now I understood why SARA charged such steep dues and conference fees. Luckily, as the Cream of the Crop winner, my only cost was the price of Blake's banquet meal, a charge roughly the equivalent of a week's worth of groceries for the two of us. Either we'd eat well tonight, or we'd be chowing down on the most expensive conference chicken ever to grace a banquet hall.

I spied Paisley on her hands and knees in the far corner of the room where she was ripping open one of dozens of cartons that surrounded her and the four other women working alongside her.

"Am I glad to see you!" she said, looking up as I approached. She stood and swiped her hands across her jeans. That's when I noticed the ribbon dangling from her conference badge.

"You didn't mention you were one of the SARA winners," I said.

"Didn't I? Blame it on the Lovinia distraction. Anyway, it's my fifth." She flicked the ribbon with her finger and shrugged. "No big deal."

It would be a big deal to me. A *huge* big deal! I was surprised at how casually Paisley accepted such an honor. The SARA was to romance what the Oscar was to motion pictures.

"Anyway," she continued, "I was supposed to have a dozen volunteers to set out all these books." She indicated the other women with a nod of her head. "Only four showed up. Five, now that you're here."

"What would you like me to do?"

Paisley quickly explained that the cartons contained books written by the main conference speakers. "We need to place one of each title on every chair."

"More free books?" My tote had contained four hardcover and eight paperback titles by various romance authors attending the conference.

The other women stopped working and turned to stare at me in a way that made me feel like a visitor from a no-freebies planet. Paisley chuckled. "You really are a newbie, aren't you?"

I wasn't sure how to take that, so I shrugged and said, "I

suppose I have a lot to learn."

She quickly introduced me to the other women—two historical romance authors who write as a team, a debut paranormal romance author, and a debut romantic suspense author.

I apologized for not recognizing any of them.

"Not surprising," said one of the historical authors. "We have no support from our publisher. After six books we're still stuck in midlist hell and expect to be dropped at the end of our current contract."

"We keep hoping our next book will break out and hit a bestseller list," said her partner, "but it never happens. Sales are dismal. Our last book didn't even make it into the chain stores. That's the death knell for us."

"My book won't be released for another few weeks," said the paranormal romance author, "and I'm already worried."

"Me, too," said the romantic suspense author. "It's a hell of a way to make a living. Word of advice, Gracie: don't quit your day job."

Too late for that. My day job already quit me.

A loud boom from above abruptly interrupted our conversation. We all gazed upward, expecting to find a gaping hole in the ceiling but couldn't spot so much as a pinhole. "What are they doing up there?" I asked.

"Making a racket," said Paisley. "I hope they're not working over the weekend. Can you imagine trying to give a workshop with all this construction noise going on overhead?"

"I guess that's why we scored such a cut-rate deal," said one of the historical authors.

Cut-rate? Yowza! I'd checked the conference fee and room

rates on the SARA website when I first learned I'd won the Cream of the Crop Award. The Friday evening through Sunday afternoon conference cost over a thousand dollars, and a basic room was three hundred and fifty dollars a night. Hardly what I'd call cut-rate!

The racket above returned to its previous level, and I joined the others on the floor to begin ripping open cartons. If we wanted time to shower and change after working in the ballroom, we had exactly an hour and a half to place one copy of each of five hardcover titles on every chair in the room. One thousand chairs times five books per chair divided by six volunteers equaled nowhere near enough time.

Once we'd opened all the cartons, we lined them up in five rows, one title per row. We then raced across the rows, grabbing a book from each carton. Beginning at the far end of the ballroom, we'd dash to a table, load the books onto a chair, then race back for another armload.

Within twenty minutes droplets of sweat gathered along my hairline and dripped down my cleavage. Not only would I need time to shower, I'd need time to wash and blow-dry my hair. "I haven't engaged in such vigorous exercise since pushing out my twins," I told Paisley as I dumped another armload of books onto a chair and stopped to catch my breath.

"How long ago was that?"

"Nearly two decades."

She gave my size six figure a quick once-over. "Well, you certainly don't look like you never exercise. Spreading bottoms are the bane of all authors because we spend too much time sitting at our computers. I hate to exercise, but if I didn't clock five miles a day on my treadmill, I'd look like a short, squat Lovinia within a week."

Yet another Lovinia comment. The woman appeared to be the main topic of conversation at the conference. "I'm getting the impression people don't like her very much."

Paisley patted my arm. "You're a quick study, Gracie Elliott. I doubt you'll find anyone here who thinks highly of the woman. You witnessed a classic Lovinia performance in the lobby earlier."

"I can't imagine she acts that way around her fans. They'd stop buying her books." I'd already decided not to purchase another Lovinia Darling romance after seeing her in action this afternoon.

"Lovinia keeps her fans at a distance to make herself appear more mysterious. She doesn't do book signings or personal appearances. The hoi polloi are beneath her."

"Yet she's here."

"Only because she's one of the founding members of SARA. She has lifetime membership privileges and likes to lord it over everyone. Besides, this is a professional conference, not a readers' convention. No fans allowed."

Or unpublished authors, for that matter. My inclusion at the conference was a special perk of my contest win. I wouldn't be allowed to join SARA until I sold my first book. That sale couldn't be to just any publisher, either. It had to be to one of a select group of publishers that met certain SARA standards. These included being in business for a certain number of years, offering an advance of at least five thousand dollars per book, and publishing a minimum number of romances each year. Any publisher not meeting these requirements wasn't considered a legitimate romance publisher by SARA.

When I began writing, I thought a career as a novelist would be an ideal substitute for my newly unemployed self. However, I was quickly learning this was as cutthroat an industry as the one from which I'd recently been booted. Maybe more so. Selling my book was only the beginning and no guarantee of success.

"Anyway," said Paisley, changing the subject back to the chore at hand, "Back to work. Think about all the calories you're burning. I know I'm going to enjoy every drop of champagne and each delectable morsel of tonight's decadent dessert without feeling an ounce of guilt."

She had me at champagne and decadent dessert. I scooped up another batch of books and headed for the next table.

~*~

An hour and a half later, as a hotel employee removed the last of the empty cartons, we surveyed our work. "Thank you, all," said Paisley, high-fiving everyone. "I couldn't have pulled this off without your help. Now let's get ready to party!"

We were walking toward the exit when the doors swung open and Lovinia Darling entered. Her brows knit together as she glowered left, then right, scoping out the tables. When she spied us, she stormed across the room, but it's hard to storm when your feet are squeezed into those Lorelai glitter pumps with their four-inch stiletto heels, and you've spent the last several hours getting sloshed at the hotel bar. She stumbled twice, both times grabbing onto chair backs to break her fall and tipping over two chairs in the process.

"This is outrageous!" she said as she stopped in front of us. She grabbed the pink Bird of Paradise napkin from the nearest place setting and flung it to the floor. Two of the books from the corresponding chair joined the napkin before she came to her own book and slapped it onto the now bare plate, rattling the glasses, china, and cutlery. "As the founder of this organization, my books are to be displayed prominently, not hidden on a chair." She glared down her nose at the much shorter Paisley. "You know that!"

Paisley glared back. "What I know is that you're only one of ten founding members, and the Board has deemed that no founding member should receive special treatment over any other founding member."

"How dare you!"

"I dare." Paisley turned to the rest of us. "Let's go, ladies. Our work here is done."

One by one we sidestepped Lovinia, but as I passed her, she reached out and grabbed my arm. I inhaled a gasp along with a major whiff of bourbon. "You!" she said, spewing spittle and booze-breath in my face. "Place my books on the table. The rest of you, help her."

Was she kidding? I jerked out of her grasp and stepped backwards. "I don't take orders from you."

Lovinia arched her back and thrust out her massive chest. "Do you know who I am?"

"Yes, I do. You're a bully."

"How dare you! No one talks to me like that. I'll see you never sell another book. You can count on—" She stopped short and focused her attention across the room. "What are you staring at?"

THREE

We all turned. Blake stood at the ballroom entrance, arms crossed over his chest. "I'm staring at my wife not being intimidated by a woman with an ego the size of Madison Square Garden." Then he spoke directly to me. "Gracie, it's getting late. You'd better hurry if you want enough time to get ready for dinner."

"I was just leaving." I nodded to Paisley and the other volunteers. "We were all just leaving."

As the six of us followed Blake out of the ballroom, leaving a gape-mouthed Lovinia to stew, Gretchen, one of the two historical authors, said, "Is that drop-dead gorgeous hunk your husband, Gracie?"

Paisley answered before I could respond. "Gracie shares a bed with her own personal cover model. Isn't he to-die-for dreamy?"

"I want him on the cover of my next book," said Gretchen. "Bare-chested and in a kilt."

"Ditto," said Shonda, her co-author.

"And me," added Samantha, the romantic suspense author.

Finally, Justine, the paranormal author, chimed in. "How absolutely studlicious! He'd make for a great vampire."

"Get in line, ladies," said Gretchen. "I called dibs first. Think he'd ever consider it, Gracie?"

Blake, walking several feet ahead of us, stepped up his pace as the back of his neck and his ears flushed a deep red. Apparently, my husband elicits the same response from middle-aged romance authors as he does eighteen-year-old coeds—drool at first sight.

I quickly changed the subject. "What do you think Lovinia will do?" I asked Paisley.

"About you? Don't worry. She has no power, no matter what she thinks."

"I meant about the ballroom. Do you think it's safe to leave her in there? Would she dare trash the place?"

Paisley snorted. "That would require effort on her part. Other than tossing her weight around, a napkin and a few books are pretty much the extent of her physical exertion. I'm guessing she exited by one of the other doors and is already making her way back to the bar."

"Shouldn't one of us go back and clean up after her?" I asked.

"Don't worry about it," said Paisley. "I'll slip in a few minutes early in case someone on the catering staff hasn't already taken care of it."

~*~

An hour later Blake and I followed a crowd of ultra-blinged-out women of all ages, shapes, and sizes into the ballroom. "The combined Miss America and Miss Universe pageants don't feature this many sequins and rhinestones," I whispered to Blake.

I'd donned a Donna Karan black silk cocktail dress that I paired with Christian Dior black suede and faux leopard print pointed toe pumps, my last shoe splurge before my forced retirement. My only bling was the one-carat diamond engagement ring on my finger. "I'm totally underdressed for this crowd."

Although it hardly mattered. No one would pay me much attention, not with Blake at my side, even if he only wore a conservative charcoal gray suit instead of the designer tuxes sported by the handful of other men filing into the ballroom.

Along the route from our room, several women had stopped to ask Blake if he was a cover model. One even pressed her publisher's card into his hand after she scribbled the art director's name on the back of it. "You must promise me you'll call her. You're absolutely perfect for the cover of my new series."

I should have thought to pin a sign to his back: "Not a cover model and not interested in becoming one."

Then again, with us down to one income and having college tuition for two kids, maybe I needed to shift my perspective on the situation and farm Blake out. Why shouldn't he consider it? Didn't Fabio make big bucks in his heyday? He'd even parlayed his cover model fame into margarine commercials and a quasi-film career. When it came to hunkalicious sex appeal and drop-dead gorgeous good looks, my Blake left Fabio in his dust.

A conversation was definitely in order.

But did I want half-dressed sexy female models getting up-close and personal with my husband during endless photo shoots? Weren't starry-eyed freshmen who constantly threw themselves at him enough of a problem?

On second thought, I'd rather earn extra money by uploading my entire designer purse and shoe collections on eBay than tempt fate. Not that I thought Blake would ever stray, but why place the man in such an awkward position?

Besides, there was the university to consider. If Blake worried about them finding out I write romance, imagine the repercussions if the president or dean or one of the trustees happened to spy Blake in all his bare-chested glory staring out from a bookstore shelf? We'd plunge from one guaranteed salary to none in the blink of an eye, not to mention the loss of our medical insurance, his pension, and paid vacations.

Scratch the cover model idea.

When I picked up my conference badge earlier, I was also given a card specifying Blake and I were assigned to the Contest Chair's table. We made our way through the swarms of people to the front of the room where the table was situated near the podium. Several women had already taken their seats, including Paisley. Blake and I joined them, placing the books from our chairs under the table as the others had.

A short, stocky, forty-something woman who wore a glittery lavender caftan, a tiara perched atop her Scarlett O'Hara ebony sausage curls, and a wide grin stood and extended her hand to me. "Welcome," she said in a thick Southern drawl as she squinted behind rhinestone-studded purple iridescent glasses to read my badge.

"Gracie Elliott!" Her grin grew even wider as she vigorously pumped my hand. "I'm so happy to meet you. I'm Hyacinth Flowers, the contest chair."

"Happy to meet you, too," I said.

Still holding my hand with both of hers she continued, "I positively adored your manuscript, sugar, and I can't wait to see it published."

Published? Did she know something I didn't? In my exuberance I started to blubber. Hyacinth spared me from making more of a fool of myself than I already had by quickly cutting me short to introduce the other women at the table, all winners of SARA's various awards for the best published romances of the year.

When she got to Paisley, this year's recipient of the Romantic Comedy Award, she said, "And this is my dear friend and conference roommate Paisley Prentiss."

"We've already met," said Paisley. "Gracie was kind enough to help me set out the books for tonight's dinner." She pulled a face before adding, "Several of my volunteers never showed up this afternoon."

Hyacinth placed her hand on Paisley's shoulder and said, "You poor dear! And with all the stress you've been under lately. Who were those no-shows? I'd like to give them a piece of my mind."

"As much as I appreciate the gesture," said Paisley, "it's probably best not to make waves."

"I suppose...still..." Hyacinth shook her head as she made a tsking sound with her tongue. Then she turned to me and said, "You have no idea what a godsend you were to our dear Paisley, Gracie. The writing gods will surely look kindly on you for your generous spirit."

"Paisley is the one who did me a favor by inviting me to join her."

"Don't sell yourself short," said Paisley. "Not everyone is willing to roll up their sleeves and get sweaty hauling around thousands of books, especially only a few hours before attending a formal dinner."

I turned to Paisley. "I'm glad I was able to help out, given whatever it is that's got you stressed." Of course, my butinsky gene horned its way into the conversation, and I couldn't help but ask,

"Are you having problems with your latest manuscript?"

I found it hard to believe that Paisley Prentiss ever dealt with writer's block, cardboard characters, or plot holes like mere writing mortals. Her action was fast-paced with characters that leaped off the page, dialogue that was never bland, and stories that grabbed the reader from page one and never let go. I doubted her books even needed much editing—if any.

"No," she said, "Although the situation is taking quite a bit of my time, more than anticipated, and that's cutting into my writing schedule." She hesitated for a moment, then explained, "My father died a few months ago, and I've been dealing with cleaning out his house to get it ready to sell."

"By yourself?"

She nodded. "I have no siblings, and my mother died when I was quite young. It was always just Dad and I. Sorting through a lifetime of acquisitions and papers is a daunting and time-consuming task, not to mention quite overwhelming. Dad kept everything. I had no idea how much he had squirreled away in cartons in the attic and basement. At times I feel like I'm on an archeological dig."

"Your husband isn't helping you?"

"He's good with the manual labor, but I have to make all the decisions regarding what to save, what to donate, and what to toss. I've barely made a dent so far, though, mostly because I keep getting caught up in Dad's writing."

"Was he also an author?"

"A math teacher, which makes finding out he kept journals that had nothing to do with theorems and equations that much more surprising. He detailed every aspect of his life—our life. I had no idea. I'm learning all sorts of things I never knew, especially about my mother."

"I keep telling Paisley she should publish them," said Hyacinth, "or use them as the basis for a memoir or an exposé."

"Exposé?"

Paisley shot Hyacinth a look that immediately precipitated a change of subject. Given the direction the conversation had taken, I hadn't yet had the opportunity to introduce Blake, who had remained silent throughout this discussion. However, I had noticed Hyacinth continually glancing in his direction. Now she turned to him and asked, "Which author was lucky enough to score you for her cover?"

Even in the dim ballroom lighting I saw the blush creep up Blake's neck and into his cheeks. "This is my husband Blake," I said. "He's not a cover model." He will *never* be a cover model.

"Really?" Hyacinth executed an exaggerated pout. "What a shame. You might want to consider it," she told Blake. "With your looks and physique, publishers would clamor for you on their romance covers." She turned to the others at the table. "Am I not right, ladies?"

Heads bobbed in agreement.

"So we've been told," I said, "but I'm afraid Blake's profession prohibits that sort of exposure."

One of the other women tittered. "No pun intended?"

Holy double-entendre! As Blake's blush deepened another three shades, I felt a conflagration burst across my own cheeks. Time for another change of subject. I turned to Hyacinth, and before discretion planted my teeth firmly in my tongue, asked, "Is Hyacinth Flowers your real name or a pen name?"

She laughed. "My real name, sugar. But wouldn't you agree it's perfect for a writer of sweet romance?"

"I do."

"Good thing she doesn't write gritty romantic suspense," said Paisley. "She'd definitely have to take a pen name for that. Tell her about your siblings, Hyacinth."

"More flowers?" I asked.

Hyacinth nodded. "Mama spent decades as the president of the Macon Garden Club." "She named her five daughters after her favorite flowers: Hyacinth, Gardenia, Magnolia, Camellia, and Peony."

"Any brothers?" I asked.

"One. Field. He's the baby."

"Field Flowers?"

"The Third. But he prefers to go by Trey."

Apparently, he didn't appreciate his mother's sense of humor. At that point the remainder of our tablemates had arrived. As Hyacinth introduced us to the newcomers, the wait-staff began pouring wine and serving the first course, a spinach salad garnished with goat cheese, raspberries, and slivered almonds and dressed in champagne vinaigrette. No one made any further comment about Blake as potential romance book arm candy.

Then again, that was probably because everyone's attention was drawn to Lovinia Darling as she made her grand entrance into the ballroom. At the sight of her, a hush fell over the room.

Lovinia looked like a one-woman Mardi Gras parade. Yard upon yard of rainbow-hued, tie-dyed chiffon fanned out from an empire waist and swirled around her Amazonian figure. The plunging neckline showed far too much cleavage for a woman who had left middle age behind decades ago. Age-spotted, crepe-skinned décolletage is best left hidden behind higher necklines.

The Bohemian chic La Maison Emilio Pucci gown was

designed for a twenty-something who weighed ninety pounds dripping wet, not a woman topping the scales at more than twice that many pounds. I envisioned poor Emilio turning over in his grave.

Lovinia sashayed around the room like Miss America strutting the catwalk for the first time after her crowning—that is, if Miss America had spent the past several hours in a threesome with Hiram and Johnnie Walker.

As she passed each table, she executed a sloppy version of the traditional beauty pageant wave—*Elbow, elbow, wrist, wrist. Touch your pearls and blow a kiss.* She lacked only a scepter and sash. And a steady gait.

I was glad she passed with her back to our table, instead concentrating her attention on the women at the table to our left. After standing up to her earlier, I now preferred to keep a low profile, avoiding any additional contact with the woman.

The last thing I wanted was for a thousand romance authors and assorted agents and editors to witness Lovinia Darling directing one of her diatribes at me—especially the agents and editors. What kind of damage might that do to my budding career?

Even though Paisley had assured me Lovinia wielded no true power, I didn't want myself in a position where I'd have to test the veracity of her statement. For that reason, I kept my head down, only darting an occasional quick sideways peek at the farcical performance.

Lovinia's strut back and forth around the ballroom lasted an excruciating five minutes, during which an awkward silence enveloped the room. When she finally arrived at the founders' table, situated in front of the podium, I twisted in my seat for a better view. A table of women sat between the founders' table and ours, providing me cover from Lovinia's inebriated gaze.

With a final pageant wave to the entire room, she plopped onto her chair, nearly toppling backwards. Luckily, one of the waiters stood inches away. He reached out in time to steady the chair and prevent her from winding up sprawled on the floor under a sea of chiffon.

Not skipping a beat, the waiter then removed the Bird of Paradise napkin from her plate and with an exaggerated flourish, unfolded it and placed it on her lap. Then he asked in a voice loud enough for the entire room to hear, "Lovinia Darling?"

Without looking at the man she gave him a dismissive wave of her hand and said, "I don't give autographs."

"Quite all right." He pulled an envelope from inside his jacket and slapped it into her extended palm. "You've been served."

FOUR

A synchronized gasp escaped from a thousand onlookers and filled the room. Oblivious to the response, Lovinia flicked the envelope toward the center of the table where it landed amid the hydrangeas. "Apparently, you're not only deaf, you're blind as a bat. I told you, I don't do autographs, and I most certainly have *not* been served." She stabbed an index finger at her empty plate. "Do you see a salad on the table in front of me?"

"I can't figure out if she's clueless, stupid, or a cunning fox that knows how to outsmart the hounds," Hyacinth drawled to no one in particular.

"All three," answered the redheaded woman seated to my right who had been introduced earlier as Natasha Burke, winner of SARA's debut author award.

The rest of the women at our table giggled, but by this time the entire room had erupted in a buzz of chatter. After what I'd overheard in the elevator earlier, I had a pretty good idea as to the topic of conversation at each of the tables.

Just to be certain, I said, "I overheard some women in the elevator saying Lovinia had been accused of plagiarism. More than once. Is that true?"

"Of course, it's true," said Hyacinth. "And this time the charges are going to stick."

"They never have before," said the woman introduced as this year's winner in the Historical Romance category. She took a sip of wine before continuing. "I don't know how she does it, but each time she manages to make the complaint disappear."

"Along with the complainant," said Paisley. "Every one of her accusers over the years has never been heard from again. At least not in the romance genre."

"Making such accusations is the kiss of death in publishing," said the winner of the Paranormal Romance award as she stabbed a forkful of salad. "No publisher wants to deal with a potential troublemaker. You never know what accusation they'll hurl next. Or at whom."

"True," said the Inspirational Romance category winner. "If these authors are still writing romance, they've probably taken on new pen names and are keeping a low profile, but I'll bet they've changed genres."

"Or they've settled out of court for a large sum of money tied to an air-tight gag order," said Natasha. "Lovinia certainly has the bank account to make her problems disappear."

"Not this time," said Hyacinth. She waved her fork at us. "Mark my words, ladies, Lovinia Darling's days as Queen of Romance are numbered. The woman is about to be toppled from her throne, and bless her thieving heart, it couldn't happen to a more deserving author."

"You say that as if you have some inside information," said

Blake, joining the conversation for the first time.

Hyacinth offered him a catbird smile. Her eyes twinkled as brightly as her rhinestone-studded glasses. "Maybe I do."

Lovinia continued to dominate the topic of conversation for the remainder of the first course and throughout the main course, a surf-and-turf of filet mignon and lobster tail with grilled asparagus and twice-baked potatoes—which certainly explained the cost of Blake's dinner. SARA spared no expense when it came to feeding its members.

As we feasted, the various authors around the table took turns sharing Lovinia tales. Many had more than one. None had any love for the woman. Part of me felt sorry for Lovinia Darling. How awful to have such a reputation, but she'd brought it upon herself by the way she treated her fellow authors. What good was all that fame and money if no one liked you? Give me love and poverty over hatred and wealth any day.

As the wait-staff removed the remains of dinner, the president of SARA stepped onto the dais and up to the podium to welcome everyone. Then she introduced the founders. One by one the ten women stood as their names were called, each receiving a generous round of applause. All except the tenth member—Lovinia Darling. When she rose, she offered the room another one of her beauty pageant waves but received a less than enthusiastic response. A few people scattered around the room made a half-hearted effort to clap, but a buzz of conversation drowned out the smattering of applause.

When the president quickly segued into introducing the current Board of Directors, the conversation died down, and the applause picked up. However, Lovinia remained standing. She turned toward the podium and glared at the president.

The president ignored her, continuing with the remaining introductions. "And finally, last but certainly not least, I'd like to introduce SARA's contest chair, Hyacinth Flowers, a woman who for the past five years has taken on the daunting task of coordinating both the annual SARA Awards for Outstanding Romance Fiction and the Cream of the Crop Award for Unpublished Romance Fiction."

Hyacinth rose and, accompanied by rousing applause, made her way up the steps to the podium. "Thank you, Madam President," she said as the president turned the mic over to her and stepped aside.

Lovinia continued to stand, still glaring at the president. Hyacinth turned to her and smiled. "Bless your heart, Lovinia, I'm humbled by your standing ovation."

The room erupted in laughter.

This caught Lovinia by surprise, but she quickly recovered. "Why on earth would I give *you* a standing ovation?"

"Because you so admire me?"

Lovinia snorted.

Hyacinth shrugged. "Then I suggest you sit down so we can proceed with the awards."

"You mean the *rigged* awards, don't you, Hyacinth?"

"Are you accusing me of something, Lovinia?"

"I certainly am."

"Why, because you haven't won in years?"

"Exactly. It's obvious you've been tampering with the results."

The color drained from Hyacinth's face, then rushed back in a purple wave of rage that matched her outfit. She looked like Lovinia had physically slapped her. Hyacinth gripped the podium as she fought to control her emotions. I imagined her silently counting to a hundred before she finally spoke. "I've. Done. No. Such. Thing."

"And I'm supposed to believe that? I sell more books than all of you put together."

Hyacinth composed herself further, continuing in a modulated tone. "We're more like the Academy Awards, Lovinia. Huge box office receipts rarely result in an Oscar. The reason you never win has nothing to do with sales and everything to do with attitude. Didn't your mama ever teach you the Golden Rule?"

"What's that supposed to mean?"

"Do unto others. You treat people like dirt. That's why they don't vote for you."

"How dare you! No one slanders me and gets away with it." Lovinia pointed her index finger at Hyacinth. "You'll be hearing from my lawyers."

"Will they have time? After all, they're going to be extremely busy saving your ass from another plagiarism suit."

"I have no idea what you're talking about. No one is suing me. I'm going to sue you."

"No one is suing you? Really? Perhaps you should read the contents of the subpoena you tossed into the centerpiece earlier."

One of the other women at the table retrieved the envelope and handed it to Lovinia. However, instead of opening it, Lovinia proceeded to tear the envelope into confetti and toss the scraps of paper in Hyacinth's direction. She then stumbled her way toward the nearest exit, bumping into half a dozen chairs and nearly falling into several laps.

Hyacinth lifted an imaginary wine glass and waved it in the direction of Lovinia's departing back. "See you at the bar, sugar."

Under his breath I heard Blake mutter, "Wow!" I didn't need

to glance in his direction to know he was giving me *The Look*.

Once Lovinia vacated the ballroom, the buzz eventually tapered off, and Hyacinth began to present the various awards. "I'd like to begin with this year's Cream of the Crop Award," she said as the waiters began serving dessert along with coffee and tea. "I've read many unpublished manuscripts during my tenure as SARA's contest chairperson, and I have to say, I've rarely come across one that moved me the way this story did. I found myself laughing one moment, crying the next. I loved both the plot and the characters and found the writing quite polished, especially for an author who first sat down to write a romance novel a little more than a year ago. I'm thrilled that our judges agreed with me.

"I'm happy to present this year's Cream of the Crop Award to Gracie Elliott, writing as Emma Carlyle, for her contemporary romance *Hooking Mr. Right*."

Applause filled the room. Applause for *me*. Even though I knew I'd already won, at the sound of a thousand pairs of hands clapping, my nerves got the better of me. I was about to stand in front of the *real* cream of the crop to accept my award. All those published romance authors, women whose books filled bookstore shelves around the world, women whose names routinely appeared on the *New York Times* and *USA Today* bestseller lists, women whose novels had been turned into television series and movies filled this ballroom.

It hadn't occurred to me to prepare an acceptance speech. Being the first award-winner called to the podium, I had no indication of what I should or shouldn't do. Utter a short, gracious thank-you and scurry back to my seat? Or was I expected to say something about my book? I'd received no prior instructions.

I froze at the thought of making a fool of myself. What if I forgot my heroine's name? And then I realized I had! *What was my heroine's name?* I couldn't remember. All my brain cells suddenly took off for parts unknown.

My heart pounded as loudly as a kettledrum during the *1812 Overture,* while my legs morphed into overcooked linguine. I reached for Blake's shoulder to steady myself. He stopped clapping and placed a hand over mine, giving it a squeeze. Our eyes met, and the love and pride I saw on his face inched the needle on my Panic Meter from Cataclysmic Anxiety Attack down to a few degrees south of Full-blown Paralysis.

I took a deep breath and zeroed in on my designer faux leopard heels. Why couldn't I have a penchant for designer running shoes instead of stilettos? Silently, I ordered my four-inch Diors not to betray me. How humiliating to trip over my own two feet as I made my way from the table to the dais!

With forced deliberation, I placed one foot in front of the other. The short distance seemed to take forever, but I finally arrived at the steps without losing my balance or my pride. Clutching the railing for dear life, I hoisted myself up the three steps.

So far, so good. I let go of the railing and took a step. The dais bounced under my feet.

"Careful," said Hyacinth. "The hotel gave us the trampoline model."

Great! My middle name is Klutz. I regained hold of the railing and slipped off my heels. "Better safe than sorry," I said as a few people in the audience laughed. I didn't care. I'd rather have them laugh at my bare feet than a graceless pratfall.

Hyacinth nodded her approval as she handed me my award, a small walnut cube that held a crystal inkwell with feathered quill.

An engraved bronze plaque attached to the base spelled out the name of the award, the year, my name, and the title of my manuscript.

After a photographer snapped a picture of the two of us, Hyacinth nudged me toward the mic and whispered, "Just a few short words of thanks will do."

I breathed a huge sigh of relief, especially since I still couldn't remember my heroine's name. Come to think of it, I couldn't remember my hero's name, either.

I stepped to the center of the podium and looked out across the room at the sea of romance authors. Then I zeroed in on my own table. Somehow through tears of joy, I managed to make eye contact with Paisley. She offered me a thumbs-up. I then looked over at Blake. A huge smile filled his face.

I took another deep breath and began. "Wow! This is so cool! Thank you, Hyacinth. And thank you, judges, whoever you are, for singling out my manuscript as this year's Cream of the Crop winner. You've taken me one step closer to fulfilling my dream of joining your ranks as a published romance author."

I scurried off the dais to the sound of more applause. As I reached the table, Hyacinth called my name. I turned to face her. "Aren't you forgetting something?" she asked.

I looked down at the award, still in my hand. "I don't think so."

A few women closest to the dais giggled. One left her seat, scooped up my shoes, and waved them in the air. That's when the entire room burst into laughter.

My cheeks flamed.

"By the way," said Hyacinth, "did I mention Gracie's book is a romantic *comedy*?"

More laughter.

Good grief! I wanted to leave an impression on these women, but as a writer, not a scatterbrained buffoon! Now I'd probably go down in the annals of SARA history as *The Writer Who Forgot Her Shoes*.

Red-faced, I slinked over to the dais to retrieve my heels. On my way back to the table I spotted a flutter of tie-dyed rainbow chiffon peeking out from behind a row of tall potted ferns that blocked the service entrance from view.

FIVE

Hyacinth resumed presenting the remaining awards. First up, the award for Best Romantic Suspense Novel. The recipient made a show of kicking off her heels and marching barefoot across the dais to the podium. Before giving her acceptance speech she said, "We all agreed Gracie had the right idea, so we're starting a new trend— barefoot award acceptance." She waved her shoes in the air over her head. "Besides, my tootsies are killing me." Laughter and applause greeted her pronouncement.

One by one the other authors at my table accepted their awards *sans* shoes, and I noticed people at many of the surrounding tables slipping out of their own footwear. My embarrassment swiftly disappeared. I turned to Blake and said, "You can eat your words now."

"Maybe they're not all mean-spirited prima donnas."

"Speaking of which," I said, "don't look now, but Lovinia Darling is hiding behind the foliage over there." I nodded in the direction of the ferns.

Blake turned toward the plants.

I batted his sleeve. "I said don't look!"

He shrugged. "That woman has serious issues."

"I'll say. Fame seems to have gone to her head."

"How do you know she wasn't always like that?"

"I suppose I don't, but I'll never let fame turn me into a monster."

"Damn right you won't," said Blake, attempting a look of overbearing menace and failing miserably.

I clamped my hand over my mouth to squelch the laughter threatening to erupt inside me.

"You two remind me of my parents," said Natasha.

I turned to stare at her. The woman had to be in her mid-thirties if she was a day. Perhaps even older. Blake and I certainly weren't old enough to have a daughter her age. Besides, we both looked at least ten years younger than our chronological ages. Everyone said so.

True, Blake had turned prematurely silver early in our relationship—probably due in part to putting up with his ditz of a wife who boogies to the tune of her own band—but neither of us sported any wrinkles or sagging jowls. "I hope that's a compliment," I said.

"Definitely." Then she changed the subject. "Did I hear you say Lovinia was lurking behind the potted plants?"

"Either Lovinia or someone wearing the same Pucci outfit. How likely is that?"

"Not likely at all. I suppose I should gird myself for a scene. Not that I didn't expect one."

"What do you mean?" asked Blake.

"Lovinia and I have history."

"We're quickly learning there are few people in SARA who don't have history with her," I said.

Natasha pulled a face. "Mine is quite different from all the others."

I wondered if she was one of the authors who had sued Lovinia in the past or even the author currently suing her, but I had no time to ask. At that moment Hyacinth announced the final award, calling Natasha's name as the winner of the Debut Author of the Year Award.

Natasha rose and headed for the podium. She forgot to kick off her heels at the top of the steps, but I chalked that up to a greater concern currently weighing on her mind. Lovinia Darling had stepped out from behind the ferns. Good thing she wasn't carrying a weapon because at that moment, she'd become the poster child for *If Looks Could Kill*, and her laser gaze had honed in on Natasha.

After Natasha gave a short acceptance speech and stepped off the dais, SARA's president returned to the mic. "Thank you once again for all your hard work, Hyacinth. This concludes our awards ceremony for the year and also signals the end of the banquet. Please leave the ballroom as quickly as possible so that the waitstaff can prepare the room for tomorrow's luncheon."

A thousand women, along with the few men in the room, rose and made a mad dash for the exits. I lost track of both Lovinia and Natasha in the crowd. Whatever their issues, I hoped Natasha was able to steer clear of the Queen of Romance. Even without knowing the nature of the history they shared, my guess was Lovinia was the root of the problem. Natasha shouldn't have her evening marred by a confrontation.

Blake and I were halfway to an exit when I felt a tap on my

shoulder. I turned around to find Paisley behind me.

"A group of us are getting together at the bar," she said. "Why don't the two of you join us? My agent and editor will be there. I'll introduce you to them, Gracie. With the way Hyacinth raved about your manuscript, you just might beat the odds and sell your book this weekend."

With a carrot like that dangling in front of me, how could I decline? Such an invitation coming from Paisley Prentiss was more than generous, especially since writing in the same sub-genre technically made us competitors. Not that Paisley needed to worry about me, a raw newbie without a single sale. "I'd love to!"

"Why don't you go without me?" said Blake. "I still have plenty of exams to grade."

"You don't mind?"

"Of course not. Husbands get in the way, remember?" He winked at Paisley, then gave my cheek a quick peck before we separated.

"If you don't hold on tight to that man," said Paisley, "I know several dozen women who will swoop down and scoop him up for their very own personal Prince Charming."

"Plenty have been trying for years."

She raised both eyebrows. "Oh?"

"Blake has been fending off college coeds throughout his academic career." I offered her a wide grin. "I was the freshman who caught him."

Paisley's eyes grew wide. "You are definitely full of surprises, Gracie Elliott." She linked her arm through mine. "The first round is on me."

One of Paisley's friends had managed to secure a large table in the bar. With more than a dozen women crowded around the long rectangular table and the bar jammed with too many people to count, a deep roar of noise filled the room. I strained to hear the conversations flying back and forth. Most of the time I found myself nodding in agreement, even though I had no clue as to the topic of conversation or exactly what I was agreeing to. Not only had I not caught most of the women's names, the dim bar lighting made it impossible to read nametags, even those on the women seated next to and directly across from me.

True to her word, though, Paisley introduced me to her agent and editor when they arrived. "Gracie, this is Dagmar Whittier, my fabulous agent, and Audra Clarke, the best editor in the business. Ladies, Gracie Elliott, winner of this year's Cream of the Crop Award."

Somewhere between their late-thirties and mid-forties, both women exuded the air of the quintessential New York career woman, dressed head-to-toe in black designer everything and sporting the latest trendy hairstyle from the celebrity stylist du jour. Having once walked among their ranks, I recognized the look and even had a good idea which stylist had last trimmed their hair.

Both pulled up chairs next to either side of me, squeezing into an already overcrowded space. "Tell us about your book," shouted Dagmar over the din of clinking glasses and numerous flying conversations.

My two critique partners had forced me to memorize what they called an elevator pitch. "It's something you can spout off in a few seconds if an agent or editor standing on line for the elevator strikes up a conversation," said Myra Fitzgerald, the only one of us who had scored an agent. "You don't want to miss a golden opportunity by becoming tongue-tied."

"What's the title again?" asked Audra.

"*Hooking Mr. Right.*"

She waved her hand for me to proceed.

Halfway into my second frozen raspberry margarita, my nerves had relaxed enough that I forgot about forgetting my hero and heroine's names. I took a deep breath and silently begged the romance writing gods and goddesses not to fail me. "Thea Chandler, a total failure when it comes to relationships, is secretly bestselling romance guru Dr. Trulee Lovejoy. Much to his dismay, Luke Bennett has been dubbed Manhattan's most eligible bachelor, and hordes of women throughout New York are using Thea's books to try to snare him. When Luke and Thea accidentally meet, he believes he's finally found an honest woman, but Thea has more secrets than the CIA and a desperate gossip columnist out to expose her. Can a butt-ugly alley cat named Cupid bring together two people driven apart by secrets and lies?"

I held my breath. I hadn't forgotten any essential details, and I hadn't stumbled over my words. I'd scored a major victory, in my opinion, but my efforts would result in total defeat if neither the agent nor the editor expressed interest in seeing the manuscript.

"Have you read any of it?" Dagmar asked Paisley.

"Not yet. Gracie and I only met earlier today on the hotel registration line."

She nodded. "Well, the proof is in the pudding, as they say." Dagmar turned to Audra. "You interested?"

"I'd be willing to take a look if the book lives up to Hyacinth's hype. You know how much I respect her opinion."

Dagmar pulled a business card from a Chanel purse and handed it to me. "Email me a synopsis and the complete manuscript."

"Thank you. I'll get it off to you first thing Monday morning."

I waited for a card from the editor; however, both women stood to leave with nothing more than a wave goodbye to Paisley. At the last moment, though, her editor turned back. I crossed my fingers and toes, hoping for a manuscript request, but instead of saying anything to me, she pointed a finger at Paisley and said, "A little birdie told me you're way behind on your latest book. You will meet your deadline, won't you?"

Paisley offered her a wide smile. "The Dagmar birdie has no reason to worry, and neither do you."

Paisley's editor nodded before followed her agent out of the bar.

I stared at their departing backs. Once they disappeared into the crowd, I turned to Paisley. "I don't understand. Your editor said she'd take a look at my manuscript. Why didn't she give me her business card?"

Paisley patted my shoulder. "She only accepts agented material. If Dagmar likes what she reads and signs you as a client, she'll send your book off to Audra."

"Oh." I felt the air slowly leaking out of my happiness balloon. I hadn't realized that was how things worked. "Do all editors only accept submissions from agents?"

"For the most part. At least those at the major publishing houses."

I still had quite a bit to learn about the publishing industry. However, my chances of getting published seemed to dwindle with each new piece of information I gleaned.

"Remember what I told you, Gracie. It's a process."

I drained the remainder of my margarita and frowned into the empty glass. "Right. A process," I mumbled. One that now appeared highly unlikely to occur in enough time to replenish my lost pension fund.

Two glasses of wine at dinner plus two frozen margaritas had filled my bladder to capacity. "I'm off to the little girls' room," I told Paisley.

"I'll order you another while you're gone."

I waved the offer away. "I'm well beyond my limit for the night."

"Nonsense. It's not like you have to drive home."

"I may need a designated walker to escort me to my room at this rate."

Paisley laughed. "I'll keep your seat warm. Hurry back."

Easier said than done. The line waiting to enter the ladies' room stretched halfway into the lobby. My bladder wasn't going to hold out long enough for me to secure a stall. I decided to take the escalator up one flight to the mezzanine level.

Once upstairs I followed the signage that pointed me toward the left, then down a hallway to the right. I was about to enter the ladies' room when I heard two familiar voices coming from around the next corner.

"Did you think if you wrote under a pen name I wouldn't find out?" asked Lovinia.

"I don't see why it's any of your business," said Natasha.

Lovinia snorted. "Oh you don't, do you? We have a contract."

"So?"

"So I own you. Everything you write, you write for me and only for me, whether you're calling yourself Nitza Burkowsky or Natasha Burke."

Natasha Burke was writing Lovinia's books?

"There's nothing in my contract that prevents me from writing my own books. I wouldn't have signed it had there been such a clause."

"Isn't there? Maybe you should have read the fine print. You have two choices: either you sign your advance and all your royalties over to me, or we go to court, and all the money you earn on that book will be eaten up in attorney fees."

"Lovinia, you can't do that!"

"Can't I? Try me."

"I swear, Lovinia, you do this, and I'll spill all your secrets. Every single one of them."

"You'll never get the chance. I'm off to call my lawyers to slap you with a gag order."

The sound of heels clicking against the marble floor grew louder. Either Lovinia or Natasha was headed my way. I ducked into the ladies' room before either spied me spying on them.

I waited five minutes after doing my business before leaving the ladies' room. Both Lovinia and Natasha were probably long gone, but I wasn't about to take any chances.

Returning to the bar, I found a third margarita on the table in front of my chair.

"Drink up," said Paisley when I protested. "You deserve to celebrate." Then she got a good look at me and asked, "What's up? You have the most perplexed expression on your face."

"I'm not sure I should say anything."

"About what?"

"A conversation I just overheard."

"Gossip? Dish, girl! You owe me. Didn't I secure you a manuscript request from my agent?"

I glanced around the noisy room. I'd have to shout to be heard over all the other conversations flying around me, and this was not news I wanted to broadcast via stretched vocal chords. "I suppose one way or another the caca is about to hit the fan. Not here, though. Let's go somewhere less crowded."

"Give up our seats? This better be good, Gracie."

"Trust me. It's beyond good."

Paisley thought for moment, weighing whether whatever gossip I might impart trumped the loss of our bar seats. Finally, Paisley stood, the lure of juicy gossip having won out. "Okay, then. But you'd better deliver."

We grabbed our drinks, and she followed me into the lobby. "Where to?" she asked.

The lobby held the overflow from the bar. Assuming we could even find a couple of seats, anyone might overhear our conversation. "Upstairs," I said. "We can duck into one of the meeting rooms."

We threaded our way through the various groups of people congregating in the lobby, deliberately avoiding Lovinia, who was currently embroiled in an altercation with Penelope McGregor. As in the event earlier that morning, Lovinia's assistant seemed to be trying to placate Penelope. From our vantage point, it looked like he was again soundly rebuffing her efforts.

When Paisley and I arrived at the escalator leading to the mezzanine level, we discovered it was no longer working for some reason. Just my luck! Paisley hiked up the skirt of her black, silver, and gold paisley print A-line ball gown with her free hand and quickly darted up the uneven metal steps, not spilling a drop of her drink along the way. She hadn't had to worry about also juggling a purse because her gold leather Valentino was a shoulder bag.

My classic black Fendi clutch came without a strap. I shoved the purse under my armpit and gingerly navigated one step at a time, clutching the rubber railing with one hand and my margarita with my other hand. Given the amount of alcohol I'd consumed and my innate klutziness, I envisioned myself tripping on the steps and spilling my drink. Somehow I manage to do neither and let loose a huge sigh of relief upon reaching the top.

"Where to?" asked Paisley once I joined her.

I guided her through several corridors to a small, out of the way meeting room and closed the door behind us after we entered.

"All this cloak and dagger," she said, settling into one of the chairs around a small conference table. "This must be some primo gossip."

I took the seat next to her. "You better believe it." I then proceeded to divulge the bombshell I'd learned about Lovinia Darling.

Paisley's eyes widened. She whistled under her breath. "Natasha is Lovinia's *ghostwriter*?"

"That's what it sounded like, which explains how Lovinia can write over a dozen books a year."

Paisley drained her glass before saying, "Plenty of authors are that prolific."

"Really? It took me more than a year to write my book."

"We all write at different speeds. The bigger question is how many books, if any, is Lovinia herself writing? Does Natasha write all of them? Or is she one of a stable of ghostwriters Lovinia employs?"

"And how long has this been going on?" I asked. "Is it possible Lovinia has used ghostwriters her entire career?"

"The plot thickens," said Paisley.

"But why would anyone agree to write for Lovinia instead of having a career of her own?"

Paisley shrugged. "Money. I'll bet Lovinia pays very well for those books—and for the authors' silence."

Another possibility occurred to me. "Or maybe she's blackmailing the authors."

"Over what?"

I thought about Sidney Mandelbaum, a client of my now defunct Relatively Speaking matchmaking service for senior citizens. Sid's deep, dark secret life led to his murder. "Everyone has secrets. Some people go to all sorts of extremes to make sure theirs stay hidden and are never exposed."

Paisley grew thoughtful. "I suppose that's true." Then she yawned. "I should probably call it a night. I have to give a workshop at nine o'clock tomorrow morning, and I really wanted to put in a few hours on my manuscript before going to bed. Dagmar and Audra have no idea how far behind I really am."

"Will you make your deadline?"

"I hope so. Deadlines always have a little padding built in, but this book is giving me fits."

I glanced up at the wall-mounted clock at the front of the room and gasped. "I had no idea it was so late. Blake is going to think I ran off with one of the cover models."

Paisley snorted. "If this were a scene in a romance novel, it would never fly. Not when you have your very own cover model waiting upstairs warming your bed."

"True. And if I'm lucky, he's still awake."

As we headed toward the elevator, I hesitated at the entrance to the stairwell. "I'm going to hoof it. Five flights might just walk off some of those calories I scarfed down tonight."

Paisley zeroed in on my Diors. "If you don't trip and kill yourself along the way. I saw how cautiously you walked up the escalator a few minutes ago."

"Because I'm a klutz and also didn't want to risk spilling my drink." I had left my untouched margarita sitting on the conference table in the meeting room. "I won't be balancing a drink this time. Besides, if I can work off a hundred calories, it's worth the risk."

Paisley started to object, but I assured her. "I'll take my time."

"Be careful, Gracie." She waved goodbye and continued toward the bank of elevators.

As I hauled myself up the first set of steps, that old adage about the road to hell being paved with good intentions popped into my head. Maybe this wasn't such a good idea, especially given all the alcohol I'd consumed over the course of the evening.

By the time I reached the first landing, my heart pounded and my pulse raced. Jeez! Was I ever out of shape! I leaned up against the wall to catch my breath and wondered how many calories I'd burned climbing one flight of stairs. Probably nowhere near the number of calories in a frozen margarita. While I waited for my heart to slow down to normal, I pulled out my iPhone to ask Siri, only to discover I had no cell service in the stairwell.

I slipped my phone back inside my clutch bag. At least five minutes passed before I'd regained enough energy to continue. Grabbing hold of the railing, I inhaled a deep breath of fortitude and started my ascent up the next flight. No matter the number of calories, I was burning more than if I copped out and took the elevator the remainder of the way.

Halfway up the third set of stairs I heard what sounded like the fire door slamming open against the concrete-block wall of the stairwell. A split second later a bloodcurdling scream echoed above me. I looked up to find a billowing mass of tie-dyed rainbow chiffon plummeting toward me. As I flattened myself against the wall, Lovinia Darling's body landed with a bone-shattering thud at my feet.

SIX

I didn't need a degree in forensics to know Lovinia Darling was dead. The top half of her body sprawled upside-down on the steps in front of me, her lower half splayed across the landing above. Dull, lifeless eyes stared up at me. Blood flowed from a large gash in her skull where her head had hit the metal edge of the concrete step and dripped toward me. I quickly descended two steps to avoid the spatter.

My entire body shook as realization hit me. If I'd rested a second less on the landing earlier, Lovinia would have fallen directly on top of me, most likely killing us both.

I'd already come too close to death once this year, thanks to Sidney Mandelbaum. Once was more than one time too many, but did the universe take my needs into consideration? I stared at Lovinia. Apparently not.

I fought to keep my legs from collapsing under me. I knew I had to move. My phone didn't work in the stairwell. Holding onto the railing for dear life, I inched my way back down the stairs to the floor below.

Once in the corridor, I crumbled into a heap on the floor. This particular corridor was in mid-remodel, the carpet already pulled up but new flooring not yet laid. I was too freaked out and tired to care about the plaster dust and assorted yuck covering the bare concrete and the damage it might do to my favorite little black dress. I fumbled for my phone, and with unsteady hands, managed to call 911.

After one ring the call was answered by someone saying, "911. State your emergency."

I'd only called 911 once in my life, but I'd never spoken a word to the operator. At the time I was being kidnapped. Luckily, my kidnapper had no idea my phone was in my pocket and not in my purse. I convinced him to allow me to use the bathroom before he dragged me out of my house. It was either that or mess up the seat of his Pathfinder. Even though he never took his eyes off me, thanks to the pony wall and frosted glass that separated the toilet from the tub, he only saw a blurry image of the top of my head. He had no clue I'd slipped the phone from my pocket, set it to silent, and dialed 911.

This time I actually had to speak to the person on the other end of the phone. Coherently. Hardly an easy task, given the current mix of margaritas and adrenaline coursing through my system—not to mention the very real possibility of hyperventilating. Why is there never a brown paper bag around when you need one?

"I'm at the Crown Jewel Hotel," I said. "I was in the stairwell, walking upstairs. A woman fell from the landing above me. She's dead."

"How do you know she's dead, ma'am?"

Was he kidding? Dare I tell him this wasn't my first encounter with a corpse? Probably not the best idea. Instead, I said, "Uhm...by the way she *looks*?"

"Are you with the victim, ma'am?"

"No. Not any more. My phone didn't work in the stairwell. I'm on the floor below."

"Is anyone else with you?"

"No."

"Do you know which stairwell?"

"What do you mean?"

"Which side of the building?"

"The stairs to the left of the lobby elevators."

"I'm dispatching EMS. They'll be there shortly, but I need you to put down your phone, check to see if the victim is breathing, then come back to tell me."

"I just told you she's dead."

"Are you a medical professional, ma'am?"

"No."

"Then please do this for me. Time is of the essence."

No way was I leaving my iPhone on the floor of the hotel. However, to humor the guy on the other end of the line, I opened the door and stepped back into the stairwell. After a few deep breaths, I grabbed onto the handrail and returned to Lovinia's body.

She hadn't moved. Her eyes still stared blankly upward. Blood still oozed from the huge gash on the side of her head, which was tilted at a very unnatural angle. In my unprofessional opinion, along with her other injuries, Lovinia's neck was broken. I stared at her chest, searching for evidence of even the slightest rise and fall but saw none.

However, since I was a trooper and just to be a thousand percent certain, I removed a compact from my clutch bag. Trying my darnedest to avoid stepping on Lovinia or in her blood, I bent over her upside-down body and held the mirror directly over her nose and mouth. I counted to three, withdrew the mirror, and checked it. No fogging.

No, I wasn't a medical professional, but again, in my extremely *unprofessional* assessment, Lovinia Darling was very much dead. If not, she was a vampire. Although some of the SARA paranormal romance authors might hold to that theory, I didn't believe in woo-woo, voodoo, or any other form of alternate reality. Lovinia Darling was dead—with a capital D-E-A-D.

I returned to the hallway and said as much to the operator— minus the vampire stuff—but he was no longer on the line. I'd disconnected the call when I stepped back into the stairwell. Oops!

I placed another call to 911 and was told to stay at my current location. Not a problem. I slipped out of my shoes, slumped onto the floor—my dress already probably ruined from my previous encounter with plaster dust and assorted grime—and didn't bother stifling a loud yawn. Who would hear me, anyway?

I must have fallen asleep because the next thing I remembered was someone shaking me. I opened my eyes to find a beefy hand clamped to my shoulder. "Are you the woman who called in the body on the stairwell?"

My gaze ran from the hand, up a jacket-clad arm. I craned my neck. A fuzzy Mr. Clean, complete with white bushy eyebrows but minus the earring and in a navy worsted suit, stared down at me. After I blinked away the fuzziness, his frowning countenance came into focus. Not Mr. Clean, his doppelganger. I nodded.

"I'm Detective Dwayne Vanslootenberger."

Hopefully he'd hand me a business card because no way would I ever remember that name, not after an evening of wine and margaritas—not to mention coming face-to-face with a dead Lovinia.

He lowered his hand to my forearm and pulled me to my feet. "And you are?"

"Gracie." My name came out as a squeak. I cleared my throat and tried again. "Gracie Elliott."

Detective Vanwhatshisname started to pull me toward the elevator. "Come with me, Gracie Elliott."

I dug in my stocking-clad heels. He narrowed his eyes and scowled. "My shoes," I said, swiveling my neck in search of my Dior pumps, which I was not about to leave sitting in the middle of a construction site.

Spying them against the opposite wall, I pointed. The detective released my arm and allowed me to retrieve my heels. Before slipping into them, I brushed away the detritus that had collected on the bottoms of my feet. Then the detective once again took hold of my arm and escorted me toward the elevator.

The detective had secured one of the hotel meeting rooms for my interrogation...uhm...statement. At least he didn't question me in the stairwell near Lovinia's body. I also had a place to sit that was far more comfortable than a cold concrete step or a grimy hallway floor.

After we took seats opposite each other at a small rectangular conference table, he reached into his breast pocket and pulled out a spiral notebook and a pencil. "How well did you know the victim, Mrs. Elliott?"

"Me?" I shook my head. "Not at all."

He zeroed in on the conference badge hanging from a ribbon around my neck. "Aren't you one of the authors at this event?"

I explained my attendance at the conference. "I've heard of Lovinia Darling, of course. She's known—or was known—as the Queen of Romance, but the only time our paths ever crossed—prior to her nearly crashing down on me, that is—was earlier today when I was helping set up for the dinner this evening." Then I remembered today was now yesterday and corrected my timeline.

"Exactly how did your paths cross?"

I told him how Lovinia had entered the ballroom and demanded I place her books prominently on the tables, not on the chairs.

"And did you?"

"No, the banquet chairperson said not to, that the Board had decided no author should be singled out for special treatment."

"What happened next?"

"We all left to get ready for the dinner."

"The victim, too?"

"No, just those of us who were setting up for the banquet. Lovinia remained inside the ballroom."

"And that was the last time you saw the victim alive?"

"No, she attended the banquet. Later that evening when I went to the ladies' room, I overheard her arguing with someone. I recognized her voice but didn't actually see her."

"Why is that?"

Duh? Was he kidding? "I didn't want to get caught snooping."

He asked me to relate the conversation I'd overheard. When I'd finished, he asked, "And the name of the other person?"

I hesitated, not wanting to get Natasha in trouble.

"Mrs. Elliott?"

"Natasha Burke."

He scribbled Natasha's name in his notebook. "And afterwards?"

"I used the ladies' room, then returned to the bar but didn't stay long. I was walking up to my room when Lovinia fell from the floor above and landed at my feet."

"Why were you in the stairwell? Why not take the elevator?"

"I wanted to burn off some of the calories I'd consumed at dinner and in the bar afterwards."

He narrowed his gaze and assessed me in a way I found exceedingly uncomfortable. "How much have you had to drink this evening, Mrs. Elliott?"

I ran a mental tab. I knew I'd had more to drink than normal, given that normal for me was generally no more than an occasional glass of wine. Or two. Definitely no more than three. Generally. Most of the time. Finally, I said, "Two glasses of wine at dinner and three frozen margaritas afterwards. No, two."

"Which is it? Two or three?"

"Two. I was served three, but I only drank two of them." When he raised his eyebrows, I explained. "I really didn't want the third margarita, but someone ordered it for me when I left the bar to go to the ladies' room."

He scrawled something in his little notebook, which made me feel my alcohol consumption needed further explanation. "The drinks were over the course of six hours, not all at once." I'll admit to having a bit of a buzz—well, maybe a little more than a bit, given I'd fallen asleep on the hotel floor—but I'm of legal age and wasn't behind the wheel of a car, so what's the big deal? Besides, those margaritas contained mostly fruit juice and ice.

He leaned over the side of the table and pointed to my feet.

"And you decided to hike up how many flights of stairs in those shoes?"

"Five and I told you why." Did he have any idea how many calories were in a frozen margarita? Apparently not.

He frowned as he scrawled something else in his notebook. That's when I segued from cooperative witness to nervous witness. "Hey, Lovinia tripped and fell down a flight of stairs. I just happened to be the unfortunate person she almost landed on."

"If you say so."

"Exactly what are you getting at, Detective?"

"Just doing my job, ma'am. You didn't see or hear anyone else on the landing above you?"

"No. Like I said, I heard the door slam open. I looked up, and a moment later Lovinia plummeted toward me." I thought for a moment. "I think maybe I heard her gasp." Or was I remembering the sound of my own gasp as my life flashed before me?

Then a disturbing thought took shape in my mind. What if Lovinia's death wasn't an accident? "You don't think someone pushed her, do you?"

"You tell me."

"I told you I didn't know the woman. Besides, if someone pushed her, wouldn't the hotel's surveillance cameras catch it?"

The detective snorted. "The hotel's system is in the process of an upgrade. Cameras on that floor aren't online yet."

"Kind of serendipitous, don't you think? What are the odds a killer would know there were no working cameras on Lovinia's floor?"

He issued another snort. "Tell me what you do know about the victim, Mrs. Elliott. Anything you may have seen or heard. I'll do the detective work."

"Even gossip?"

He nodded.

I attempted to stifle a yawn but failed miserably. "Sorry. I heard several people mention Lovinia spent most of yesterday in the bar. Judging from her behavior, she was obviously already drunk when she entered the ballroom last night."

"In what way?"

I explained her performance. "I wouldn't be surprised to learn she also downed quite a few glasses of wine at dinner. Her tablemates could fill you in on that. But..."

"But?"

"Again, this is all gossip. I have no firsthand knowledge of any of it."

"Go on."

"From what I gather, no one likes—liked—her, but it went way beyond that. She had enemies, including someone suing her for plagiarism."

Vanwhatshisname bent his head to scribble something in his notebook. When he finished, he raised his head and shot me one of those police glares perfected by every actor who's ever starred in a cop drama. "Were you one of her enemies?"

"Of course not! Haven't you been listening to me, Detective? I told you I'm not published, and I didn't know her. I'm here only because I won a writing contest."

I crossed my arms over my chest and glared at him. "Besides, if you think I pushed her, you need to brush up on Einstein's Theory of Relativity. How could I have pushed her down a flight of stairs, yet arrive at the spot where she landed before she did? I've told you she missed falling on top of me by mere inches. I'm not some Marvel superhero!"

"I only have your word that she nearly fell on you."

I forced out a lungful of frustration. "Right. I don't suppose there are any working cameras in the stairwell to back me up?"

He shook his head.

"Great. So you're saying you suspect foul play? And I'm a suspect? Why would I call 911 if I killed her?"

"To deflect suspicion from yourself?"

"Good grief! You can't be serious." Had I known I'd wind up in this pickle, I wouldn't have called the police in the first place. Let the next person climbing up the stairs find Lovinia. Given that she died instantly, what difference would it have made, other than saving me from a seat under the detective's microscope?

He closed his notebook and placed it in his breast pocket. "Like I said, I'm only doing my job. However, this does appear to be an unfortunate accident. The heel of the victim's shoe broke. We found it on the landing above. Most likely, that's what precipitated her fall." He stood and offered his hand. "Thank you for your cooperation, Mrs. Elliott." He reached into his pocket, pulled out a business card, and handed it to me. "If you remember anything else, you can reach me at this number."

I reached for the card. "That's it? I can go?"

He nodded. "You're free to leave."

I stared dumbfounded for a moment, not sure I'd heard correctly. "I don't get it. Why the inquisition, then? Wait." I held up my hand. "Just doing your job, right?"

"Exactly."

I always thought there was a good cop paired with a bad cop during interrogations—questionings—, but maybe the NYPD was short-staffed tonight. Or maybe I'd watched too many cop shows on TV. Either way, I saw no reason to hang around after receiving the green light to go. I stood and headed toward the door but stopped as I reached for the doorknob.

"Remember something else, Mrs. Elliott?

"No, but I'm wondering why Lovinia had entered the stairwell in the first place."

"Her room was located two doors down from fire door."

"You think she was so drunk she didn't know the difference?"

"Possibly. We found her key card on the landing near the door. Or she may have stumbled in the hallway on her way to her room and fallen into the door, pushing it open with the weight of her body. Forward momentum did the rest."

I nodded and left the room, but as I headed back to my own room, this time taking the elevator, I started to wonder whether Lovinia's death really was accidental. I searched my brain, trying to unearth some deeply buried tidbit that might indicate someone had pushed her, but the events all happened so fast. I didn't hear any arguing or even any conversation before the slamming door startled me.

Yet, so many people hated Lovinia, and for some that hatred might be reason enough to want her dead. For all I knew there were dozens more people who felt the same way about her. Had one of them silently come up from behind and pushed Lovinia to her death?

By this point it was nearly three in the morning. I expected to find Blake fast asleep when I entered our hotel room. At least I hoped he was deep in Slumberland. I needed a few hours of shut-eye before I could process what had happened and make sense of it, much less explain to my husband how his wife had once again come face-to-face with a dead body—a dead body that might have met its end through less than accidental means.

Not that anyone was currently investigating Lovinia's death as a homicide if I believed Detective Dwayne Vanwhatshisname, but maybe he wasn't being exactly truthful with me. The guy had talked out of both sides of his mouth, and I'd gotten the sense that at least one of those sides had been intent on tripping me up and finding holes in my recounting of events.

However, once again the universe was getting a good laugh at my expense because instead of finding Blake fast asleep, I found him sitting up in bed, his nose buried in a book.

"Have a good time?" he asked.

I burst into tears.

Blake tossed back the blanket and bounded out of bed. He scooped me into his arms and carried me back to the mattress. I don't know how long we sat there, him comforting me, me sobbing hysterically into his shoulder, until I eventually wore myself out, my tears leveling off from a gush to a trickle.

"What happened?" he finally asked.

"She's dead."

"Who's dead? Paisley?"

"Lovinia." I gulped in some air before my words spilled out in a less-than-coherent rush, but apparently Blake got the gist of the events. He asked no further questions, just held me close.

The next thing I knew, it was morning.

SEVEN

"You could go back to sleep," said Blake after I returned from a trip to the bathroom and headed toward the dresser.

I glanced at the bedside clock as I pulled clean underwear from a drawer. Seven o'clock. How much shut-eye had I gotten? Three hours? Four, max? It didn't matter. I was wide-awake. Sort of. I stifled a yawn before responding. "I don't want to miss any of the workshops."

Not to mention all the gossip that was certain to be swirling around Lovinia's death. Was it an unfortunate accident as Detective Vanwhatshisname had suggested? Or was it murder, as he also suggested? I wasn't exactly functioning on all cylinders this morning, thanks to too much alcohol, too little sleep, and a pounding headache that was the result of both. At this point I wasn't certain of exactly what the detective had inferred and what I'd read into his words.

Not that I knew more than an NYPD detective but my sixth

sense told me there was more to Lovinia's death than losing her balance after breaking a stiletto heel. Or perhaps that was simply my writer's brain trying to make sense out of a senseless death. One thing for certain, I needed coffee to kick-start my brain before I could coherently remember the events of last night and sort fact from fiction.

But first I needed a couple of aspirin. I returned to the bathroom to rummage through my cosmetic case in the hope of finding some.

After downing the aspirin, showering, and dressing, Blake and I headed around the corner from the Crown Jewel to a coffee shop on Lexington Avenue for a quick breakfast. The conference wasn't supplying a meal prior to the start of the morning workshops, and we weren't about to pay ten times what a coffee shop would charge for the exact same menu of juice, coffee, eggs, and toast at the hotel restaurant.

Apparently, other conference attendees had the same idea. The coffee shop, a throwback to the middle of the last century, complete with turquoise vinyl booths and yellow Formica tabletops, was filled to capacity with women I recognized from last night's banquet.

"It will be about a fifteen minute wait," said the hostess when we approached her station.

Blake gave our name, and we stepped aside to wait for a table to free up. A moment latter I saw Paisley waving us to join her at a booth toward the back of the room. We removed our name from the waiting list and made our way down the aisle where we found Paisley sitting with Hyacinth.

"Have you heard the news?" asked Paisley as I settled in beside Hyacinth and Blake took the seat next to Paisley.

Once again, I felt overdressed in my linen suit. Today I'd paired it with an unconstructed white crepe shirt and a geometric silk scarf in riotous shades of teal, plum, and emerald, from my last collection of fabric designs before receiving the pink slip that ended my career in fashion.

Hyacinth wore a pair of lavender jeans with a purple T-shirt. *Romance Writers Do it Between the Sheets* in large sequined magenta script emblazoned her ample chest. I caught Blake quickly averting his gaze and spearing me with *The Look*. Paisley, showing better taste, had dressed in business casual: khaki pants, a black T-shirt, and an earth-tone paisley print blazer.

"Do you mean about Lovinia?" I asked her.

"I always said karma would catch up with that woman," said Hyacinth, "bless her heart." (The phrase, I've learned, is most often Southern-speak for the completely opposite sentiment.) "I just never expected it to happen at one of our conferences. Or come as a result of a broken heel. Of all things! Can you imagine?"

"What do you mean?" asked Blake.

"Only that if a stiletto was going to do her in," said Hyacinth, "it would be a stiletto knife plunged into her back, not a defective shoe. With all the enemies that woman racked up over the years, I guarantee no one is shedding any tears of grief over her death."

"Maybe that's what really happened," I said.

The color drained from Hyacinth's face. "Are you suggesting someone *stabbed* Lovinia?"

"We heard she died from a fall," said Paisley. "What have you heard, Gracie?"

"I meant in a figurative way," I said. "Not that someone literally stabbed her to death."

"According to what everyone is saying," said Paisley, "her death was an accident."

"Maybe it was," I said.

"Why do I get the feeling you don't think so?" she asked.

"I'm not sure," I said, "but something just doesn't add up."

"You didn't even know her," said Hyacinth. "What do you suspect that the police don't?"

"It's not that I suspect anything; it's just a feeling."

Blake reached across the table and squeezed my hand. "My wife has a very active imagination."

"Well, we know that," said Hyacinth, peppering her words with a laugh. "It's part of the reason she won the Cream of the Crop Award—that and her fabulous writing skills." She turned to me. "Sounds like you're churning up a romantic suspense in that brain of yours, Gracie."

I shrugged. "Maybe I'm letting my imagination run amok. Chalk it up to drinking too much last night, lack of sleep, and a near-death experience."

Hyacinth gasped. "What near-death experience?"

Paisley had quirked her head and was staring at me. I could almost see the wheels turning in her brain. "You took the stairs shortly before Lovinia's body was discovered. Gracie, you're not the person who found her, are you?"

"I didn't just find her. She came within inches of flattening me."

"Oh, dear!" said Hyacinth. "You poor thing!"

Paisley placed her fork on her plate and leaned forward. "Gracie, did you see something that would lead you to believe Lovinia's death *wasn't* an accident?"

"Ready to order?" asked a waitress who at that moment appeared at our table, pencil poised over an order book. I held up a finger to Paisley, the universal signal for *hold on a sec*, while Blake and I placed our breakfast orders.

The waitress jotted down our choices, then filled our coffee cups. After adding a splash of milk, I drained my cup while the waitress refilled Paisley and Hyacinth's cups. Then I held my cup out for a refill before the waitress headed back to the kitchen.

Caffeinated enough for the time being, I answered Paisley. "No, I didn't see anyone besides Lovinia in the stairwell, but as Hyacinth pointed out a moment ago, the woman certainly had many enemies. Far too many not to investigate the possibility that her death might not have been an accident."

"For the *police* to investigate," said Blake. "*You're* not getting involved this time, Gracie."

"This time?" asked Paisley.

I bit down on my lower lip. Blake had opened the can. Time to spill the beans. "I sort of solved a murder a few months ago."

"And nearly got herself killed in the process," said Blake, shaking his head at me. "Which is why, if the police suspect foul play in Lovinia's death, they'll investigate and solve the case without your help."

"But everything we've heard this morning indicates Lovinia tripped and fell down the stairs." said Paisley. "Have you heard otherwise, Gracie?"

"The detective speculated on the possibility that someone may have pushed Lovinia."

"What detective?" asked Paisley.

"The one who interviewed me."

Hyacinth's eyes widened. "You were interviewed by the police?"

"Well, yes. I placed the 911 call."

"Why would he suggest someone killed Lovinia if he told you her death was an accident?" asked Hyacinth.

"He said it was his job to investigate all angles, including that someone may have pushed her. Given all the people who hated Lovinia, you have to admit, it's not out of the realm of possibilities."

I'd only seen Lovinia in action less than twenty-four hours and already could name several people who would rejoice in her demise. How many more were there that I didn't know about? How many of them filled with such hatred for the woman that they'd take matters into their own hands?

Paisley picked up her coffee cup and leaned back against the booth. "I suppose anything is possible, but wouldn't this hypothetical person run the risk of getting caught either by someone else on the floor or the security cameras? After all, this is New York City. There are cameras everywhere."

"The security cameras on that floor aren't operational," I said.

Paisley raised an eyebrow. "How do you know that?"

"The detective told me when I raised that very question."

"But if someone deliberately killed Lovinia," said Paisley, "how would that person know the cameras weren't working?"

I shrugged. "Beats me. Maybe it's obvious by looking at them."

"Perhaps the killer—if there is a killer—didn't know and got lucky," said Blake, "seizing upon an opportunity that presented itself and committing a crime of passion rather than a pre-meditated murder."

Paisley thought about that for a moment, then nodded. "Of course. That makes sense—*if* her death was a murder."

She turned to me. "At any rate, I want a complete word-for-word, play-by-play of your interrogation by that detective. This will be great book research."

"For what?" asked Hyacinth. "You don't write romantic suspense."

Paisley shrugged. "I might at some point. You never know."

"I wasn't interrogated," I said. "I gave a statement."

Paisley waved her hand in dismissal. "Whatever. As Nora Ephron used to say, 'It's all copy.' And this sounds like great copy for a future book."

"For a book *Gracie* should write," said Hyacinth. "It was her experience."

"It doesn't mean she can't share it," said Paisley. "I wouldn't use her words verbatim, simply learn about procedure to make sure my scenes are accurate."

"Just as long as we're clear on that," said Hyacinth. Then she patted my hand. "I can't imagine what you went through last night, you poor dear. How awful! I probably would have fainted dead away—or worse—if I'd been in your place."

Poor Hyacinth looked like she just might faint—or worse—at that moment. The little amount of color left in her face had completely drained away, leaving her as pale as the napkin she clutched in her hand. She took a sip of water and patted her chest. Hyacinth Jones was definitely no steel magnolia.

I was glad the conversation had moved on, and neither she nor Paisley had asked about the details of the murder I had previously solved. If Hyacinth learned the circumstances surrounding Sidney Mandelbaum's death and its aftermath, she might stroke out. Or kick off her heels and flatfoot it all the way back to Dixie.

The waitress returned with our breakfast orders. By this time Paisley and Hyacinth had finished eating, having arrived well before us, and the waitress handed them their checks.

Paisley glanced at her watch. "I hope you don't mind, but I've got to run. I want some time to go over my notes before my nine o'clock workshop."

"Not at all," I said. "I'll see you there as soon as we finish eating."

Blake stood to allow her to leave.

"I'll go with you," said Hyacinth. "I can save a seat for Gracie."

"Thanks!" I scooted off the banquette so Hyacinth could maneuver herself out of the booth.

Paisley took three or four steps before she stopped, turned around, and returned to the table. "Wait for me after the workshop, Gracie. I want to speak to you about something." Before I could answer, she pivoted on her heels and rushed to catch up with Hyacinth.

After Paisley and Hyacinth departed, Blake dipped his fork into his scrambled eggs and raised the utensil. "Know what this is?"

"Your breakfast?"

"A metaphor for my words." He placed the egg in his mouth. "I'm eating them. You were right."

"About what?"

"I'm afraid I judged too quickly yesterday. Some of these romance authors are genuinely nice women. I'm glad you've made some new friends."

"Hyacinth's crass T-shirt aside?"

He nodded. "I wonder if she's aware of the double-entendre."

"Oh, I'm sure she is. After all, she's a romance writer."

Blake frowned. "Promise me one thing, Gracie?"

"What?"

"You'll never write *Fifty Shades of Trash*."

"Blake Elliott! I have children and hope to have grandchildren some day. Do you think I'd want my name attached to books like that?"

He raised both eyebrows. "What about Emma Carlyle's name?"

"Emma's standards are my standards." I studied my husband's face for a moment. "Is that what you've been worrying about ever since I started writing?"

"The thought had occurred to me. I know you're trying to find some way to earn the kind of money you once made."

"Darned right, I am. I have no desire to spend my golden years living above an auto repair shop in Newark."

Blake sighed. "We're not going to wind up in some seedy apartment, Gracie. I'm a tenured professor. I'm not your father."

My father, the man who couldn't hold down a job. By the time I was in my teens he'd been fired from so many positions that I'd lost count. We rarely had the proverbial two nickels to rub together, let alone money for even the smallest of luxuries. Maybe that explains my designer shoe and handbag compulsion, a compulsion from which I've had to go cold turkey since losing my job. It also explains why, even though Blake makes a decent salary, I have a need to make an equal or better one.

Dad finally got anger management counseling in his fifties and learned how to bite his tongue instead of telling off his bosses. This enabled my parents to have a relatively comfortable life until he died a few years ago. Luckily, he left mom with a decent life-insurance policy. Needless to say, though, I've known poor, and I never want to go there again, thank you very much.

"And don't forget," added Blake, pulling me out from my morose remembrances, "we currently have two kids in college.

That won't last forever."

"Still, now that I think about it, those *Fifty Shades* books have sold millions of copies."

"Gracie..." Blake shot me *The Look*.

"How does *Fifty Shades of Recyclables* sound?"

EIGHT

Once we finished our breakfast, Blake and I returned to the Crown Jewel. While I attended workshops, he planned to finish grading exams, then work on his future Pulitzer Prize-winning book, *Pop Goes the Culture,* his epic tome on twentieth century culture and counter-culture and its influences on the media.

"Why don't you grab your laptop and find a quiet spot in the business center?" I suggested, wrinkling my nose at the thought of my husband spending one second more than necessary in our sorry excuse for a room. "Or camp out poolside on the rooftop deck."

"I don't mind the room," he said. Blake found the mid-century modern décor charmingly retro. All I could see were decades and decades of germs lurking in every nook and cranny.

"Do it for me, then. I won't enjoy myself worrying an army of antibiotic-resistant bacteria and other assorted microscopic organisms are spending the day feasting on you."

"We could have gone home last night, Gracie. You can't have it both ways."

"I don't see why not." Although, had we spent the night at home in our own bed, I wouldn't have experienced that near-death experience from a plummeting Lovinia. Or its aftermath.

~*~

When I arrived at the meeting room assigned to Paisley's workshop, I was glad Hyacinth had offered to save me a seat. The room was jam-packed with authors. Some women even sat on the floor along both sides of the room. Others leaned against the back wall. What a testament to Paisley's popularity among her fellow authors. Would these women one day feel the same way about me? If only!

I spotted Hyacinth's ebony sausage curls toward the front of the room. Good to her word, she'd claimed the chair next to her by depositing her purse and canvas tote bag on it. When she saw me, she freed up the chair and patted the seat. I squeezed into the row and joined her just as the workshop hostess began her introduction of Paisley.

Pulling a notebook and pen from my own tote bag, I settled into my seat, my nerves tingling in anticipation of the information I'd glean from Paisley's vast reservoir of knowledge and experience.

I suppose, given that the SARA conference was for published authors, I shouldn't have expected to find workshops that would help me hone my writing skills. However, Paisley's presentation yanked the Sarouk right out from under me. Not the double-whammy I wanted after having only moments earlier dredged up those painful childhood memories of poverty.

Entitled "The New Normal", in many ways the workshop was an extension of the downer of a conversation from the day before when I met the other authors who had volunteered to set out books for the banquet. I suddenly realized I'd entered the world of publishing at the worst possible moment. My heart sank into my stomach as Paisley ticked off all the recent publishing mergers, which precipitated lines folding, scores of editors receiving pink slips, and more and more authors finding themselves orphaned.

As a result, many previously published authors were now striding down a once shunned path. "Years ago we looked with disdain at people who self-published," said Paisley. "But that was back when self-publishing was the last resort for poorly written books that no legitimate publisher would purchase. Desperate would-be authors turned to unscrupulous vanity presses just to get their names on the spine of a book. Times have changed, ladies."

She paused to scan the audience. "How many of you have been cut by your publisher this year?"

Nearly half the women in the room raised a hand.

"How many of you have had success moving to another publisher?"

All but three women lowered their hands.

Paisley shook her head. "I'm afraid what we're experiencing is only the tip of a Titanic-sinking iceberg. It will get worse. However, we now have options not available to us previously. Over the last few years many authors have begun to take charge of their own careers and are now making as much or more money by going out on their own."

"Are you suggesting we walk away from traditional publishing?" asked one author seated several rows behind me.

"I'm suggesting you consider and take advantage of all your options," said Paisley.

"What about you?" asked a second woman seated across the aisle from me. "Are you willing to walk away from your publisher?"

"No," said Paisley. "I'm not suggesting any of you do that. As long as my agent can secure me equitable contract terms and decent advances, I'll continue with my publisher—or any other publisher who might want to sign me. But I don't have a crystal ball. I can't know how long my publisher will continue to support me, or if another publisher will want me, should I find myself without a contract.

"For that reason, I decided awhile back that it was time to place a foot in both worlds. Eight months ago I secured the rights to my out-of-print backlist and published those titles myself. The results? I've doubled my income for the year—all from books my publisher had decided the public no longer wanted to read. Well, guess what? The public has proven the publisher wrong."

"That's great for you," said another woman. "You have a huge fan base. What about those of us who are not a permanent fixture on the *New York Times* Bestseller List?"

Paisley shrugged. "What do you have to lose? If you've been cut by your publisher and haven't found another who will publish you, why not try going out on your own?"

"And if our publisher isn't willing to give us back our rights or we don't have much of a backlist, then what?"

"Write a new book. Publish that one on your own."

"Who's going to buy a book I publish myself? I'm a virtual nobody. I had a two-book contract before I was cut."

"People bought those books, didn't they?" asked Paisley.

The woman nodded.

"Did you receive good reviews?"

"Good reviews but my publisher did absolutely zilch in the way of promotion, and my book never got placement in the big box stores."

"So you didn't earn out your advance?"

"You got it."

"Many of the people who read and liked your books will buy your new one," said Paisley. "They won't care that you've published it yourself. Most of them won't even realize the book isn't from a traditional publisher. How many of you realized that my backlist is now published by me and not my publisher?"

I glanced around the room. Besides Hyacinth, only four other hands shot up, and like Hyacinth, they all knew Paisley personally. I recognized the four women from the bar last night.

"She's right," said a woman in the front row. "There are people who have never had a traditional publishing contract who are now selling thousands and thousands of books online. We all know word-of-mouth is what really sells books. A good book will find an audience. Maybe not overnight, but you've all seen what can happen when readers start talking about a specific title."

"Books by well respected publishers," said one woman.

"Really?" said another. "Where have you been the last few years? I can name dozens of self-published books that have made it big, and those authors never had a publishing contract."

"If you polled readers, asking who published their favorite books," said Paisley, "I'm willing to bet they wouldn't be able to tell you. *Authors* check out a book's publisher, not the general public. They don't know one publisher from the next."

A woman sitting on the floor at the side of the room stood and said, "I've heard bookstores are reluctant to shelve self-published books."

"Not totally true," said Paisley. "They won't stock books they can't return for credit if the books don't sell. However, they will fill customer orders for books they don't carry. Bookstores do that all the time. No bookstore is large enough to carry every published title. Besides, more and more readers now buy their books online. They have to. Look at all the bookstores that have closed over the last ten years."

"Here's something else to consider," said the woman in the front row who had spoken earlier. "Maybe you won't sell as many copies on your own as you did with your publisher, but you'll be making seventy percent on each sale instead of the ten percent your publisher paid you."

"Paisley makes a lot of sense," added a woman seated to my right. "Why ignore a potential revenue stream? I know the first thing I'm going to do when I get home. I'm calling my agent and telling her to demand my rights back. I've got titles that have been out of print for years."

The longer I listened, the more depressed I became. "Where does this leave someone like me?" I whispered to Hyacinth.

She patted my hand. "It's not all doom and gloom, Gracie. Publishers are still buying books from new authors. It's just not as easy as it once was because there are fewer publishers and fewer places to sell books. Then when you do sell, the advances most publishers are offering are nowhere near what they used to be, often as low as ten percent of what they were twenty years ago."

She patted my hand again, then gave it a squeeze. "You wrote a great book. I'm convinced you'll be one of the success stories."

Would I? I certainly hoped Hyacinth had her own crystal ball into the future—or at least a more positive insight into the future of publishing. However, something told me I'd make more money asking, "Do you want fries with that?" than I'd ever make from selling *Hooking Mr. Right*.

By the end of Paisley's forty-five minute presentation I was wallowing in an ocean of self-pity. First, my fabulous job gets outsourced to a third-world nation. Then my brilliant entrepreneurial venture into the world of senior citizen matchmaking goes belly-up with the murder of Client Number Thirteen, Sidney Mandelbaum. Now I discover I've spent over a year working on a novel that will earn me pennies—assuming it ever sells at all.

How lucky can one girl get?

Paisley wrapped up her presentation to a standing ovation from her fellow authors. While women still clapped, Hyacinth darted out to her next workshop, once again promising to save a seat for me. I remained in my chair, nursing my crushed ego, while a horde of authors swarmed Paisley. I listened as they picked her brain further about her successful foray into the world of self-publishing.

Eventually, the room cleared out as women rushed to other presentations or retook their seats in preparation for the next speaker to appear in that room.

"Let's find a quiet place to get some coffee and talk," said Paisley, approaching me.

"About what?"

"You, of course."

Paisley gave no other clue about the topic of conversation as I followed her down the elevator, through the lobby, and out of the hotel. She led me back to where we'd eaten breakfast. "Perfect," she said, scouting the now near-empty coffee shop. "The breakfast crowd is gone, and it's too early for the lunch crowd. We can talk without fear of any nosey authors or anyone else listening in on our conversation."

With my curiosity spiking off the charts, I scooted into one of the turquoise vinyl booths and immediately asked, "What about me?"

Before Paisley answered, she signaled the waitress and ordered two coffees for us. As the waitress poured the coffees, Paisley asked me, "You want anything else?"

"Answers?"

"In time. And two bialys," she told the waitress.

Finally, after the waitress left to grab our bialys, Paisley said, "Last night when I returned to my room, I asked Hyacinth to email me your manuscript."

"Why?"

"She bragged so much about your story that I wanted to see it for myself."

"And?"

"I couldn't put it down. I stayed up all night reading it."

"I thought you were going to work on your manuscript."

Paisley turned sheepish. "I thought if I read something else and stopped forcing myself to write, it might rid me of my writer's block."

"Did it?"

Paisley shrugged. "Time will tell. I haven't had a chance to get back to the manuscript yet. Anyway, getting back to you—"

"Yes?" I held my breath, awaiting Paisley pronouncement.

"You've crafted a wonderful romance, Gracie. I fell in love with Thea and Luke."

High praise coming from Paisley Prentiss. If my smile grew any wider, my face might crack. I could barely contain my excitement, but somehow I managed a "thank you" without jumping out of the booth and executing a happy dance in the middle of the coffee shop.

"That's not all."

My eyes bugged out. "There's more?"

Paisley nodded. "First thing this morning I sent your manuscript to my editor."

Omigod! "Really? I thought she only accepts agented manuscripts."

"From unpublished authors, but she'll read what I send her. Besides, I'm sure my agent will be contacting you with an offer, especially if my editor loves your book as much as I do."

My heart pounded with excitement. I leaned back in the booth, closed my eyes, and inhaled a deep breath. I couldn't believe my good fortune. And all because *New York Times* bestselling author Paisley Prentiss happened to stand behind me in line at the hotel registration desk. Talk about serendipity!

"I can't believe what you've done for me, Paisley. How can I ever repay you?"

"Hey, you haven't received an offer of representation or a book contract yet. Personally, though, I think you're on your way, girl."

"But still, I wouldn't have this opportunity without your intercession." I thought about the crowded room we'd just come from, the love her fellow authors showed Paisley. Then I thought about the scorn these same women harbored for the now deceased Mean Queen of Romance. Paisley Prentiss and Lovinia Darling, two bestselling authors with completely different attitudes and temperaments. Lovinia could have learned a thing or two from Paisley. Now it was too late.

"When the time comes," said Paisley, "all I ask is that you pay it forward."

"What do you mean?"

"When I attended my first writing conference, I was as green as you, not to mention terribly shy. I knew no one. You, at least, have your husband here with you. I was sitting alone at breakfast that first morning when a woman came up to the table and asked if she could join me. I had no idea who she was, but that breakfast changed my life."

"Who was she?"

"Liz Phillips. She took me under her wing and mentored me. I owe my career to her, and the only thing she ever asked in return was that if someday I had the chance to help another author, I would do so."

"I'm honored, Paisley. I won't let you down." If I beat what seemed like insurmountable odds in today's publishing climate, I'd definitely emulate Paisley Prentiss.

"You better not!"

The waitress returned with the two plates of bialys and placed one in front of each of us. Paisley smeared hers with butter before taking a bite. Chewing around the mouthful, she said, "There was something else I'd like to discuss with you."

"I'm all-ears."

"I got to thinking about what you said this morning, about how someone may have killed Lovinia. Maybe you're right, given all the people who hated her."

"I get the feeling the detective really believes her death was purely accidental, that he only brought up the possibility of someone pushing her because it's his job to investigate all angles."

"He doesn't know any of us or Lovinia's history. The conference ends tomorrow, and we'll all scatter across the country. Maybe you and I should see if we can find out something that will point the police in the right direction."

"Blake will kill me."

Paisley winked. "He doesn't have to know. We won't do anything that will jeopardize our own safety. Besides, I have an ulterior motive..." She waited a beat, then added, "research."

"For what?"

"A book, of course. This is too good an opportunity to pass up. Everyone is talking about Lovinia's death. Someone might inadvertently drop a clue. Or at the very least, supply an interesting plot twist."

Hyacinth was right. Paisley wanted to piggyback on my traumatic experience of last night to cash in on Lovinia's death. No matter how nice Paisley had been to me, I didn't care for the idea of her picking my brain for her next bestseller. However, I had too much to lose by accusing her. Instead I said, "No one is going to admit being anywhere near Lovinia at the time of her death."

"You did."

"That's different. She nearly landed on me."

Paisley shrugged. "You'd be surprised what I've overheard in the bar during romance writing conventions and conferences. Alcohol loosens both tongues and inhibitions. If I wanted to, I could make a fortune blackmailing some of my fellow authors."

My eyes bugged out, and my jaw dropped. Paisley laughed. "Not that I ever would, of course."

"Good to know."

"It hardly matters, though. Even if the detective is right, as he most likely is, and Lovinia's death was a tragic accident, most fiction is based on a certain element of truth. What we learn by eavesdropping and engaging people in conversation could result in a bestseller for us."

"Us?" *Talk about jumping to the wrong conclusion, Gracie!*

"You mean collaborate? You and me?"

"Why not? It will be fun. Of course, the actual writing will have to wait until I finish the manuscript from hell, but we can certainly brainstorm ideas for now." She pulled a pen and a yellow legal pad from her canvas tote. "We should start by making a list of possible suspects."

"Like Natasha?"

"Given what you overheard last night, I'd say she's Suspect Number One." Paisley jotted down Natasha's name.

"I believe the detective already plans to interview her."

Paisley raised an eyebrow.

"He asked me the last time I saw Lovinia before her death. I told him about the conversation I overheard near the ladies' room."

I liked Natasha. I hated to think she might be a killer. My gut told me she wasn't. "Wouldn't Natasha have more to lose by killing Lovinia? She probably made a lot of money ghostwriting Lovinia's books."

"Not necessarily," said Paisley. "Besides, we don't know if Natasha was Lovinia's only ghostwriter. There could be others. Before last night would anyone have guessed the woman paid people to write her books for her?"

"Still, even if Natasha only wrote one or two books a year for Lovinia, all of Lovinia's books hit the bestseller lists."

"That doesn't mean Natasha benefited. I'm sure Lovinia paid her by the book, not a percentage of her royalties. I don't know anything about Natasha's personal life or her finances. What if she has huge credit card debt or is trying to stave off foreclosure on her home?"

I nodded. "Given the economy, her husband might have lost

his job or filed for bankruptcy."

"Exactly. Or perhaps he walked out on her. Who knows? Lovinia may have taken advantage of Natasha's need for money."

I reminded Paisley of the possibility I brought up last night. "Lovinia may have been blackmailing Natasha."

"When it came to Lovinia, nothing would surprise me," said Paisley. She drew a large star next to Natasha's name. "Who else?"

"You probably know more about Lovinia's enemies than I would. Who do you think might have killed her?"

"We'll get to my list in a minute. For now, let's continue with your observations from yesterday."

"Hyacinth?"

Paisley laughed. "You're joking, right? Hyacinth barely reaches five feet in heels and is nearly as wide as she is tall. She's half the size of Lovinia. I can't imagine her mustering the strength to push Lovinia down a flight of stairs."

"She might with enough adrenaline coursing through her body. Besides, last night she said Lovinia's days were numbered and insinuated that she knew something we didn't."

Paisley rolled her eyes. "I believe she meant her standing at the top of the bestseller lists. Several other authors are gaining ground on Lovinia, myself included. I think we can safely assume Hyacinth is no killer. Who else?"

Before I could answer, the waitress reappeared, topped off our coffees, and asked, "Anything else I can get you ladies?"

Paisley turned to me. "Gracie?"

"I'm good."

"Just the check," she told the waitress.

The waitress withdrew a slip from her apron pocket and placed it on the table. "No rush. Have a nice day."

I had continued to mull around Paisley's question. Only one other person stood out in my mind. "What about the person suing Lovinia for plagiarism? Too bad we don't know who that is."

"Oh yes we do," said Paisley.

"Really? I got the impression last night that no one knew."

Paisley grinned. "Not any more. The kitty is out of the sack, and Lovinia unwittingly unleashed her."

"How?"

"One of the authors sitting at Lovinia's table gathered up the torn subpoena and slipped the pieces into her purse after Lovinia stormed out of the ballroom. She and a few other authors sifted through the scraps until they found the name of the person who filed the lawsuit." Paisley jotted down a name and turned the legal pad around to show me.

"Ronelle Crenshaw? I'm not familiar with her."

"You wouldn't be. She's not published. She won the Cream of the Crop Award two years ago."

"But if she's not published, she wouldn't be at the conference. How could she have killed Lovinia?"

"It's a public hotel, Gracie. Anyone can walk through the entrance and hop on an elevator. Only the concierge floors require a special elevator key, and even that can be circumvented."

"How?"

"Easy. Say you and I are on the elevator. I have a room on a concierge floor. You don't. I insert my key card for my floor. You simply exit the elevator at the same time I do."

"But why would Ronelle Crenshaw kill Lovinia if she had just filed a lawsuit against her? If she won, she stood to walk away with a huge settlement."

"For one thing," said Paisley, "plagiarism is very hard to prove.

She had no guarantee of winning. Or perhaps, like your husband suggested, Lovinia's death was a crime of passion. Ronelle saw an opportunity and grabbed it."

I thought about that for a moment. "She may have come to the hotel to watch Lovinia served with the papers." Who would have noticed one additional woman at the back of the ballroom last night?

"Exactly. If you'd sued Lovinia for plagiarism, wouldn't you want the satisfaction of seeing the look on her face when she was handed those papers?"

"I lost my job, Paisley. I'd much rather have the satisfaction of winning a large judgment against her."

"Our suspect may have decided she preferred a more drastic form of revenge, especially after seeing Lovinia tear up that subpoena. Maybe she became so angry over Lovinia's reaction that she snapped."

"You think she kept her eye on Lovinia the rest of the evening and followed her up in the elevator later?"

"It's possible. No one would have recognized her, least of all, Lovinia. That woman was too self-absorbed to notice anyone but herself."

"Did Ronelle attend the conference two years ago when she won the award?"

Paisley nodded.

"She may have worn a disguise last night to make sure no one else recognized her."

"That makes two viable suspects," said Paisley, adding a star to Ronelle's name. "Anyone else?"

NINE

Anyone else? I nibbled on my bialy as I thought back to my first Lovinia sighting. "Yesterday she and Penelope McGregor exchanged angry words when she barreled into him as she exited the elevator. But that's hardly motive for murder unless Penelope's a psychopath."

"They have history," said Paisley. "I'm just not sure exactly what, but that incident yesterday was no fluke. Those two have been antagonistic toward each other for as long as I've known them."

"What if she tumbled down the stairs because he clobbered her with his cane, then pushed her through the door?"

"Certainly a possibility."

"Do you know Penelope well enough to feel him out?"

Paisley wrinkled her nose. "Feel him out?"

"Strike up a conversation and find a way to learn if he has an alibi for the time of Lovinia's death." All of this speculation about murder would lead nowhere if our prospective suspects had ironclad alibis that put them far from the scene of the crime last night.

"Hardly. We're certainly not friends, more like acquaintances with six degrees of separation between us. We've attended the same conferences over the years and once served on the SARA Board together. Other than that, I doubt we've ever exchanged more than a few words."

She added Penelope's name to the list, then said, "Penelope's a loner. I don't even know his real name. I'm not sure anyone does."

"The hotel would have his real name," I said, reminding Paisley of Blake's comments when stood on the registration line. "He'd have to present a photo ID at check-in."

"But they'd never give us that information."

"True. The only other person I can suggest is Lovinia's assistant."

"Marcella the Mouse?"

"Is that what people call her?"

Paisley nodded. "Fits, doesn't it? Lovinia rode roughshod over that poor woman. I have no idea why Marcella put up with the constant abuse. Certainly there are better jobs out there, especially for someone with her skills. How many people can claim they survived working for Lovinia Darling for years?"

"How long did she work for Lovinia?

"At least twelve years, as long as I've been in the industry. Perhaps longer. A better sobriquet might be Marcella the Masochist."

"Maybe she finally snapped," I said. "Victims of abuse often do."

Paisley glanced at her list. "Lots of possible snapping." She added Marcella's name. "The wonder is, if Marcella did snap, why she didn't snap sooner."

"So what about you, Paisley?" I asked. "Did you ever have a run-in with Lovinia?"

"Me? Sure."

"Enough to kill her?"

Paisley laughed. "Hey, I have an ironclad alibi. I was up all night reading your book, remember? Hyacinth is my witness." She shook her head. "No, Lovinia was an equal opportunity bully. If she hadn't died last night, once you sold your book, you, too, would have eventually wound up in her crosshairs. I don't know a single SARA author who doesn't have a Lovinia horror story. It's practically a rite of passage."

"That would make for quite a few suspects."

Paisley shrugged. "Maybe we all got together and gave her a group shove."

"Sounds like *Murder on the Orient Express*. One crime, many perpetrators." It also struck me as frighteningly similar to the motive behind Sidley Mandelbaum's murder.

"Brilliant," said Paisley. "We could call our book *Murder on the Crown Jewel Staircase*. Although we'd have to change the hotel name to avoid a possible lawsuit."

"Should we add a romance or keep it a straight suspense or mystery?"

"We're romance writers, Gracie. Besides, my readers will expect any book with my name on it to be a romance."

"So romantic suspense or romantic mystery?"

"I'm thinking sexy romantic suspense." When I raised both eyebrows, she winked at me and said, "Hey, sex sells."

"*Fifty Shades of Murder?*"

"Not a bad idea for a title, especially if we come up with fifty suspects." Paisley returned her legal pad and pen to her tote bag, glanced at the check, and pulled out her wallet. "I need to get back to the conference. I'm on a panel soon. Coffee's on me."

"Let me at least leave the tip."

She waved away my offer. "No need. You were a cheap date."

As we headed back to the hotel, Paisley pulled out her phone and said, "We should exchange numbers."

Could this day get any better? Bestselling author Paisley Prentiss wanted to give me—Gracie Elliott, wannabe romance author—her phone number? I barely contained my giddiness as I rattled off the ten digits.

~*~

We arrived back at the hotel a few minutes later and queued up for the elevator. When the doors of one car finally opened and disgorged its occupants, the line began to move, and we inched forward. However, by the time we reached the front of the line, only one more person could shoehorn into the crowded car. "You take it," I said to Paisley, since she needed to get to her panel on time.

As I waited for the next elevator, I saw Lovinia's assistant speaking with Penelope McGregor. He wore the same Home on the Range outfit he'd worn the previous day. However, unlike yesterday, today I noticed no hostility between him and Marcella. Quite the opposite, as a matter of fact. Penelope had his beefy plaid arm around Marcella's shoulders and seemed to be comforting her. After a few seconds she stepped out of his embrace, raised her thick owl-rimmed glasses from her nose, and dabbed her eyes with the wadded tissue she clutched in her hand.

The abused upset at the death of her abuser? Not that I expected to see her executing cartwheels in the Crown Jewel lobby but given the way Lovinia had treated her, Marcella's emotional display surprised me—unless it was all for show.

A luggage cart filled with several suitcases stood a few feet away from her, a bellman waiting patiently alongside it. With Lovinia dead, there was no reason for Marcella to remain at the conference. If I didn't speak with her now, I'd forfeit the opportunity.

I slipped out of the elevator line and placed myself between Marcella and the hotel exit. While waiting patiently for my chance to approach her, I discreetly studied her. She appeared even mousier than the day before with her shoulders slumped and her limp hair pulled back into a ratty ponytail. She hadn't bothered to apply even a trace of makeup to camouflage her blotchy red, tear-stained face.

After a few minutes Penelope, aided by his cane, lumbered off across the lobby. He'd only covered a short distance when he stopped and reached into his pocket, withdrawing a nebulizer. After taking a puff, he continued on his way.

I approached Marcella. "I'm so sorry about Lovinia," I said.

She glanced at my conference badge. Her face registered recognition. "Gracie Elliott. The detective mentioned your name. You're the person who found her, aren't you?"

I nodded.

She reached out and grabbed hold of both my hands, squeezing tightly. "Was she in pain? Did she say anything before she died? Call for anyone?"

"No, from what I could tell, she died instantly."

"Oh," Marcella's hands turned limp and dropped to her sides. "I thought maybe she might have..." Her voice trailed off.

"Might have what?"

She shook her head. "Nothing."

I stared at her. Was I looking at a cold-blooded murderer worried that Lovinia might have divulged her killer's name to me before she died? Why would Marcella think I'd keep such vital information to myself rather than telling Detective Vanwhatshisname when he questioned me?

If Marcella were Lovinia's killer, she wasn't thinking straight. Had I coughed up her name last night, she'd currently be cooling her sensible Easy Spirit pumps behind bars at Rikers, not standing in the Crown Jewel lobby about to depart *sans* handcuffs and on her own volition.

Besides, her features and body language projected genuine grief. At least, it looked that way to me. Then again, wouldn't a darned good actress know exactly how to behave in such a convincing manner without anyone realizing she was putting on an act?

For all I knew, Marcella Ford came to New York hoping to make it big on Broadway. She wouldn't be the first dancer or actress forced to give up the greasepaint for a steady income when her dreams of stardom didn't materialize.

Unfortunately, before I could glean any information from her, Marcella abruptly said, "I have to leave." She nodded to the bellman, then pivoted on her heels and headed for the exit.

I stared after her as she walked out onto the sidewalk and waited while the doorman hailed a cab for her. Within seconds a taxi pulled up to the curb. Marcella settled into the back seat while the bellman loaded the luggage into the trunk. A moment later the cab merged back into traffic. Opportunity lost.

As I made my way back to the bank of elevators, something niggled at the edges of my brain. I began replaying the short conversation in my head, but nothing jumped out at me.

I hated when that happened. It was like trying to remember someone's name or the title of a book or movie. I'd sense the words darting around the edges of my brain like a Quidditch golden snitch, but try as I might, I couldn't harness my inner Harry Potter to snag those elusive words and force them to the surface.

At least not until three in the morning when I'd bolt upright in bed remembering what I'd forgotten. At that point I'd be wide-awake and unable to fall back to sleep. When this happened at home, I'd get out of bed and watch a movie or fold laundry or bake a cake. If it happened tonight, I'd be stuck in a hotel room with a snoring Blake and a battalion of invisible germs plotting their attack on my sleeping husband and me.

Think positive, Gracie! Glass half-full. At least the room didn't have bedbugs.

I glanced at my watch. Paisley's panel had already started. I tapped my foot impatiently waiting for an elevator. The meeting room for Paisley's panel was only one flight above the mezzanine, but even though I wanted to get to the panel as quickly as possible, after last night the thought of entering the stairwell again gave me the heebie-jeebies.

I also wanted Blake to hear the good news about my book. The trauma of Lovinia's death had completely overtaken me last night. I had totally forgotten to tell him about Paisley's agent requesting my manuscript. Now that manuscript was also sitting in Paisley's editor's IN box. For all I knew, she might be reading it at this very moment. I could have a contract offer by the end of the weekend!

While I waited for the elevator, I debated with myself: panel or Blake? The panel won out. I was here to learn, even if what I'd learned so far had depressed the heck out of me. I needed to soak up all the publishing knowledge anyone was willing to share because I wouldn't have another opportunity like this for a very long time. Being out of work, I couldn't justify the cost of attending any other writing conferences.

When the elevator finally arrived, I stepped inside and traveled up the two stories. The doors opened, and I made my way down the hall to the meeting room featuring Paisley's panel, then quietly slipped through the doors at the back of the room. The panel, consisting of four long-time, bestselling authors, was titled "The Business End of Things" and focused on the various aspects of an author's career beyond writing publishable books.

Once again the room was filled beyond capacity. A quick scan of the seating area revealed no available chairs, not even one beside Hyacinth, who stood out from all the other women, thanks to those ebony sausage curls of hers. I suppose when I didn't show up for the last workshop, she'd given up on me.

I found a few inches of available floor and squeezed into the space between two other authors. After pulling out my notebook, I dropped my black leather Tom Ford messenger bag and conference tote bag onto the carpet between my feet and leaned against the wall for support.

Within minutes my pen couldn't keep up with all the information the panel tossed around as each member spoke. I created a column where I jotted down terms that left me clueless. My hand cramped and my brain began drowning in facts and figures.

I'd spent over twenty-five years learning the ins and outs of the textile industry. Over the course of my career I'd sat on similar panels, dispensing my knowledge to roomfuls of fashion students who had probably felt exactly the way I did right now.

I glanced down at my nearly indecipherable scribbling, hoping I'd be able to make sense of it once I returned home. Even though I belonged to a local writing group, their meetings mostly stressed ways to hone our writing skills. In the year since I'd joined, the only practical topics covered had concerned writing query letters to agents and how to pitch a book to agents and editors at conferences. Trying to learn everything else about the publishing industry in one weekend was a Herculean task, made exponentially more difficult by the awkwardness of writing while standing elbow-to-elbow with other women.

At the conclusion of the panel, the room moderator reminded everyone that the SARA business meeting would take place next, prior to lunch. As a non-member, I wasn't allowed to attend. I decided to find Blake to tell him the good news about my book. While everyone else either migrated toward the escalator or the elevator bank to descend one level to the mezzanine for the business meeting, I waited for a car heading upstairs.

Blake wasn't in our room, which was in the process of being cleaned by one of the housekeeping staff. Part of me wanted to point out all the areas in desperate need of disinfectant and elbow grease but decided not to waste my time. If the Crown Jewel cared about the cleanliness of the rooms that had not yet undergone renovation, our room would sparkle like one of the jewels in their crown.

Instead I whipped out my cell phone and called my husband. "Where are you?" I asked when he answered on the second ring.

"Poolside. I took your advice."

"Smart man. I'm on my way up."

Easier said than done. I cooled my heels for a solid ten minutes waiting for an elevator. When I finally arrived on the rooftop, I set out in search of my husband.

I'd experienced smaller country clubs. The massive rooftop deck housed an Olympic-sized swimming pool along with a separate lap pool, wading pool, and hot tub. An outdoor restaurant and bar ran the length of one side of the deck. Tables with massive shade-providing silver umbrellas circled two sides of the pools while lounge chairs upholstered in a silver and gold chevron pattern lined the other two sides. Glass walls along the outer edges of the building formed a windbreak. The facility even boasted a retractable roof, enabling the area to remain open during inclement weather.

Enormous black-glazed terra cotta pots filled with a variety of shrubbery were strategically interspersed throughout the seating areas, creating a semblance of privacy for guests but making it next to impossible for me to pinpoint Blake's location. I wandered around until I finally found him seated at a table under one of the umbrellas. His Mets baseball cap provided additional protection from the sun. Hopefully, he remembered to slather sunblock on his exposed skin. Even though the UV levels from the early May sun weren't high at street level today, forty-stories up meant forty stories closer to the damaging rays of the sun.

I glanced around but saw only his laptop on the table and nothing at his feet. Damn! I didn't want to lose my husband to skin cancer. Luckily, I always came prepared. I whipped out a tube of broad-spectrum, maximum strength SPF from my messenger bag and applied the cream liberally to my face, neck, and arms. Then I passed the tube to Blake.

He waved the sunblock away. "I applied some before coming up."

"Humor me. Add a second coat."

Blake gave me *The Look* as he lowered the lid of his laptop and reached for the tube. He could shoot me *The Look* every day for the rest of his life and seventeen times on Sunday for all I cared as long as he kept melanoma at bay.

"I have some great news," I said, changing the subject.

"Should I be worried?"

Being the pragmatic worrywart of the family, Blake often sees my good news as maybe not so good news—like when I told him (after the fact) that I'd started Relatively Speaking, my introduction service for single seniors. I'd waited until I'd signed several clients before springing the news on him. Big mistake.

After he calmed down enough to speak coherently, he said the business was a lawsuit waiting to happen. Then Sidney Mandlebaum had the temerity to get himself murdered, and Blake insisted I close up shop. For the sake of my marriage, I complied. At least he had the good sense not to say, "I told you so."

"No need to worry," I assured him. "I haven't invested our life savings in shoe umbrellas." Not that we have much in savings with two kids in college and the loss of my pension fund. "However, I still think they're a great idea."

Really, when you pay hundreds or even thousands of dollars for a pair of designer shoes, don't you want to protect them from a sudden downpour? Personally, I think the guy in Japan who invented shoe umbrellas is a genius. I have no idea why they haven't caught on in America.

Blake shook his head as he finished applying the sunblock. Then he flipped the cap closed, and handed the tube back to me. "I'm listening, Gracie. What's your good news?"

I plopped into the chair beside him and practically giggled with excitement. "Paisley Prentiss is my fairy godmother." I then told him about the agent request and how Paisley had taken it upon herself to send my manuscript to her editor.

Blake reached for both my hands. "Gracie, I'm thrilled for you." He glanced left and right, I suppose worried that the president of his university might be lurking behind one of the potted ferns and threaten to yank his tenure for cavorting with romance authors. Satisfied of his job security, Blake leaned forward and planted a quick kiss on my lips.

Then he settled back in his chair and asked, "So how's the investigation going?"

"What investigation?"

"Don't play dumb with me, Gracie. I know you too well. You and your breakfast buddies are plotting something."

I held up both my hands, warding off Blake's undeniable psychic ability. "I swear I haven't done anything other than offer my condolences to Lovinia's assistant when I saw her in the lobby earlier."

Blake leaned back, crossed his arms over his chest, and arched an eyebrow. "Why do I get the feeling there's more to it than that?"

Damn! He'd gotten into my head. "I'll admit Lovinia's death isn't sitting well with me. I keep thinking there's more to it than a simple accident. And there's something niggling away at me about Marcella, but I can't put my finger on it."

"Marcella?"

"Lovinia's assistant."

"Do you think she had something to do with Lovinia's death? I'm sure the police questioned her."

"They did, although they obviously don't suspect her."

"How do you know that?"

"She checked out of the hotel."

"If the police suspect foul play—which is a big if—they may still be putting their case together. How did she appear to you?"

"Extremely upset. She'd been crying."

"Understandable, given the circumstances."

I shrugged. "I don't know. With the way Lovinia treated her, I didn't expect Marcella to be so overwrought. Upset, yes, but her grief went well beyond that of the death of an employer, especially such a difficult employer."

"Lovinia was much more than Marcella's employer."

I stared at my husband. "What do you mean?"

"Really, Gracie? I'm surprised you didn't see it."

"See what?"

"That Lovinia and Marcella are related."

TEN

Talk about an OMG moment!

Marcella had mousy brown hair to Lovinia's platinum blonde, and Marcella was petite whereas Lovinia was Amazonian. Staring into Marcella's red-rimmed eyes earlier, I'd seen something that hadn't registered at the time but had since itched like a cerebral mosquito bite. I now realized behind those glasses with their thick lenses hid Lovinia's eyes.

Those blank green eyes had stared up at me last night and would forever be etched into my brain. I hadn't noticed the similarity earlier because yesterday I'd been focused on Lovinia throughout the drama unfolding at the hotel registration desk. I'd noticed Marcella more in terms of her body language, not any specific features. Even if I had paid more attention to her, the physical distance between us, coupled with her glasses, probably would have prevented me from getting a good look at her eyes.

However, Blake knew nothing of Lovinia's reputation as the Queen of Romance. He'd observed both women with equal impartiality and noticed what I'd missed. For that matter, what everyone else had missed, as well, given that neither Paisley nor any other author had mentioned anything about the two women being related. Who knew my husband was a budding Sherlock Holmes?

Questions played pinball inside my head, bouncing back and forth frenetically. How could all the other SARA authors, who had known Lovinia and Marcella for so many years, not see the resemblance? Many of them had come in contact with Lovinia and Marcella countless times. Did Lovinia's constant histrionics and egotistical personality overshadow her mousy assistant to the extent that everyone's focus dwelled constantly on Lovinia and *only* Lovina? Was Marcella always hidden in plain sight, swallowed up by the dark hole of Lovinia's shadow? After all, people see what they want to see. No one ever really saw Marcella because she faded into the woodwork.

This blood connection must be what caused Marcella to put up with Lovinia's crap and stay with her all those years. But if so, why keep the relationship a secret?

"Earth to Gracie."

I glanced down at Blake's hand shaking my knee. "Huh?"

"Where were you?"

"Lost on the Isle of Confusion. You're absolutely certain they're related?"

"Of course not but I saw a striking resemblance, especially—"

"In their eyes."

"That and their ears."

"Their ears?" Blake noticed Lovinia and Marcella's *ears?*

"They have the same ears."

I stared in amazement at my husband. Who notices people's

ears unless they're enormous and standing out from their heads? "Should I be worried you were checking out other women so intently?"

"Slow-moving line. The unexpected drama broke up the monotony."

"Maybe you should offer your powers of observation to Detective Vanwhatshisname."

"If he's questioned Marcella, he most likely already knows of the relationship—if there is one."

"How could there not be one with what you're telling me?"

Blake shrugged. "It could be a random genetic coincidence."

Right. And little green men from Mars built the pyramids.

My buzzing phone interrupted us. I fished it out of my messenger bag and checked the display. "I have to leave," I told Blake. "The SARA luncheon starts in fifteen minutes. My other good news will have to wait until the afternoon workshops end."

"Keeping me dangling?"

"You know what they say, Blake: always keep them coming back for more."

My husband shook his head. "Stay out of trouble, Gracie."

"I hate when you say that."

"I say it for a reason."

I knew that—which is why I hated when he said it. My husband knew me too well. Still, he really had no reason to worry. My niggling suspicions most likely stemmed from the "what if" side of my writer's brain, coupled with Paisley's suggestion that we use those suspicions to collaborate on a book. With visions of bestsellerdom dancing before my eyes, who could blame me for wanting to dig a bit deeper?

However, speculation aside, Detective Dwayne

Vanwhatshisname had chalked Lovinia's death up to a tragic accident. The cameras on Lovinia's floor may not have been working, but by now the police would have checked the elevator cameras and questioned everyone who rode up in the same car with Lovinia last night, assuming those cameras worked. At this point, with all the construction and upgrades taking place at the hotel, that was a big *if*. Also, even if Lovinia and Marcella did share DNA, it didn't prove Marcella killed Lovinia.

I headed down to the ballroom and waited with the throng of conference attendees for the luncheon doors to open. While cooling my heels, I eavesdropped on the conversations swirling around me. From what I gathered, something that occurred during the annual SARA business meeting had the makings of a major rebellion.

All around me women argued against what appeared to be a unilateral Board decision that no one outside of the Board of Directors favored. Only with all the shouting going on around me, I couldn't figure out the gist of that proposal, other than it somehow involved Lovinia Darling. Even in death the woman still wielded power over SARA and all its members.

As I glanced from one group to the next, I noticed a scowling Natasha Burke standing off to the side, observing the chaos, and inched my way toward her. When she saw me approach, she shifted her features and greeted me with a slight smile.

"What's going on?" I asked.

"The Board decided to honor Lovinia's memory by creating a scholarship in her name."

"The membership is opposed to that?"

"One hundred percent. We'd rather not have Lovinia's name attached to anything, given how she treated us."

"Wouldn't a scholarship help the membership move on and heal all the discord?"

Natasha bristled with indignation. "Absolutely not! Having Lovinia's name attached to anything will be a constant reminder of the years of havoc she wreaked and the lives she destroyed."

I saw her point, but from what I'd observed, the Board had no love for the woman, either. I pointed this out to Natasha. "It makes no sense. Why would they honor a woman even they despised?"

"Publicity. They don't want any backlash from the media if they don't do something in her name. The public has no idea how Lovinia treated her fellow authors."

"You especially?"

Natasha's featured shifted from outrage to puzzlement. "What do you mean?"

"You ghost-wrote some of her books, didn't you?"

Her jaw dropped. Her panicked eyes darted around the room, making certain no one had overheard me. Then she grabbed my arm and yanked me away from the ballroom and around the corner, out of earshot of everyone. "How did you learn about that?" she asked, keeping her voice only a decibel or two above a whisper.

I told her about overhearing her confrontation with Lovinia.

Natasha hung her head and sighed. "It's true."

"Was she blackmailing you?"

Her head shot up. "No! And I didn't kill her if that's what you're inferring."

I'm not the best actress. Natasha must have seen guilt written all over my face because she added, "Rumor has it you think Lovinia's death might not have been from an accidental fall."

"It's a working theory." When her eyes filled with fear, I added, "One that the detective in charge of the case doesn't share."

"Well, if someone did push her down those stairs, you'll have to look elsewhere to find her killer. A dozen other authors plus a cocktail waitress can vouch that I was in the bar before, during, and after her death. We saw the police and paramedics arrive, then leave a short time later with her body. We just didn't know it was Lovinia until this morning."

"If she wasn't blackmailing you to ghostwrite her books, why did you agree to do it?"

Natasha shrugged. "Why do any of us do what we do? For the money."

"But what about your own career?"

"I didn't have one at the time. Six years ago I won the Cream of the Crop contest. In my acceptance speech I mentioned how I considered myself Lovinia's greatest fan. I'd read all of her books so many times, that I'd memorized entire scenes. I credited my win to what I'd learned about writing from reading her romances."

Natasha paused, then laughed bitterly. "Of course, like every other fan of romance, I knew nothing about the real Lovinia Darling at that point, only the public persona cultivated by her publicists. I'm sure you know what I mean."

"Yes, experiencing the real Lovinia at work was a complete shock."

"My shock came later. A few days after the conference, Lovinia's assistant called and invited me to meet privately with Lovinia. Can you imagine?"

"A real fan-girl moment?"

"To be sure. However, when I arrived, before I even met Lovinia, Marcella insisted I sign a non-disclosure agreement. Not only couldn't I tell anyone what we discussed at the meeting, I couldn't even admit that a meeting had ever taken place."

"Because they wanted you to ghostwrite her books?"

Natasha nodded. "Lovinia couldn't keep up with the demands of her publishing contracts. She was getting on in years, and even though no one ever admitted to it, I believe she was either suffering from severe mental problems or in the early stages of dementia."

"Either would certainly explain her behavior. Although others have told me she's always been slightly crazy."

"Yes, but the crazy had started to hinder her ability to write. How long do you think her publisher and everyone else would put up with her antics if she could no longer churn out at least half a dozen bestsellers a year?"

"Not very long."

"Exactly. So Marcella hit on the idea of hiring someone to write for Lovinia. After hearing my acceptance speech, she finagled a copy of my manuscript from someone at SARA, liked what she read, and approached me."

"And Lovinia was on board with this? What a shock to her ego!"

"Indeed. I became a constant reminder of her new reality, that she could no longer write as she once had. She resented me, but Marcella convinced her she had no choice, that she needed me."

The Marcella I'd observed seemed to have little sway over Lovinia. I couldn't imagine how that conversation went down.

"And I needed her," added Natasha. "Or at least her money. So we put up with each other."

"Why you?"

"I was an unknown writer who knew Lovinia's style inside out.

My manuscript proved I could write. And Marcella had done her homework."

"Meaning?"

"She knew I needed money. Desperately. She made me an offer I couldn't refuse."

Even though Natasha's finances were none of my business, my curiosity trumped my manners. What did I have to lose? She could always say it was none of my business and walk away. "Why did you need money?"

She hesitated for a moment, and I could tell by her expression she was debating whether or not to answer my question. Finally she took a deep breath, then said, "A year before I won Cream of the Crop, my father suffered a massive stroke that caused permanent physical and mental damage. We had to move him into a nursing home. His medical expenses bankrupted my parents. When they lost their home, my mother moved in with me."

"I'm sorry."

"It gets worse. The stress took its toll on Mom. She suffered a series of heart attacks, each one leaving her more and more debilitated until she, too, finally had to enter the nursing home. Dad died after a year. Mom followed him a week later. And I'll be paying off their medical bills for another ten years now that Lovinia is dead."

Which definitely ruled Natasha out as Lovinia's killer. She needed Lovinia alive.

"Were you her only ghostwriter?"

Natasha nodded. "I write fast, and Marcella feared that having more than one ghostwriter ran the risk of people finding out. Someone might talk. I had good reason to keep my mouth shut."

"And you were also writing your own books?"

"When I could squeeze in time, which wasn't often."

I wondered when she slept.

"I wasn't trying to deceive Lovinia by taking a pen name," she explained. "After all, I did attend the conference and knew she'd find out when I accepted my award for Debut Author of the Year. I just never expected her to pitch a fit and threaten me."

"Does your contract preclude you from writing on your own?"

"Absolutely not. Lovinia had no basis for her threats, but she's never let facts get in her way."

By this point the din from the authors gathered around the corner had diminished. "Sounds like they opened the doors," said Natasha. "We should go."

She led the way back toward the ballroom. Once inside she put an end to any further conversation between us by taking a seat at a table with only one remaining unoccupied chair. Without a word to me as I stood inches from her, she immediately struck up a conversation with her tablemates. Subtle. I left in search of somewhere to sit.

I suppose Natasha had resented divulging her history to me. I'd picked at a fresh wound. The conversation also probably embarrassed her, given that she'd had to bare her soul to someone only once removed from total stranger status. I couldn't fault her for wanting distance between us. Still, between her alibi and her finances, I had no choice but to strike her off Paisley's list of possible suspects. Natasha lost a great deal with Lovinia's death and gained nothing by her demise.

The ballroom looked similar to the night before with the same hydrangea centerpieces in the middle of each table, but the room had taken on a less formal atmosphere. Linen bows no longer decorated the chair backs, basic white table linens had replaced the pink, and the tables were set with standard hotel silverware and white china.

I scanned the room in search of a familiar face seated at a table with at least one empty chair. Not finding any, I headed toward a half-empty table near the back of the room. After removing three more free books from an unoccupied chair and placing them in my tote, I took a seat.

The five other women at the table, all in their early to mid-twenties, interrupted their conversation long enough to offer a quick welcome but didn't bother introducing themselves after they learned I wasn't one of them—in other words not a "real" author due to my status as one of the great unpublished. I didn't recognize any of them, and the dim lighting in the room prevented me from reading the nametags hanging from ribbons around their necks.

They immediately returned to their animated conversation, leaving me alone with my half-wilted, brown-edged iceberg lettuce salad, which I proceeded to give my undivided attention. SARA had apparently blown most of their meal budget on last night's elegant repast. Odds were looking pretty good for overcooked conference chicken, limp green beans, and mushy pasta as the main course.

Talk about feeling like a fifth wheel—or more accurately a sixth, given my tablemates outnumbered me five to one. Whether they were bestselling, multi-published authors or relative unknowns, their frozen shouldered rudeness made for a stark contrast from the reception I'd received up to this point from other SARA members. If I'd had some graceful way of switching tables, I would have done so in a New York minute. I doubt they'd notice, but on the off chance they did, I refused to set myself up for possible backstabbing comments from total strangers.

Instead, I continued to pick at my salad, pretending not to eavesdrop on a version of the same conversation I suspected was occurring at every other table in the room—the newly created Lovinia Darling Memorial Scholarship Fund.

A perky blonde millennial said, "I know it's not right to speak ill of the dead, but I hated her."

"You're not alone," said another perky blonde. "That woman made my life miserable."

A freckle-faced woman with a mass of brunette curls said, "I have it on good authority that our dear overlord pressured the SARA Board into establishing the scholarship." My ears perked up as a litany of nasty comments, similar to those I'd already heard about Lovinia, segued into juicy gossip. Through hooded eyes I watched the five women, thankful for the centerpiece of hydrangeas that helped mask my spying.

"I wondered about that," said Perky Blonde Number One. "No way would they be making such a gesture out of the goodness of their own hearts. They all hated her, too."

A raven-haired woman with a frozen face that suggested recent Botox injections turned to Freckle Face. "Who told you about this?"

"Pecorino's secretary."

"On a Saturday?" asked Freckle Face.

"He called her into the office first thing this morning after hearing about Lovinia's death. She overheard his end of a phone conversation and sent me a text about it. He's anteing up the seed money."

This was no conversation between SARA authors. I hadn't taken a seat at a table of other authors; I'd plopped myself at a table with publishing professionals—and not just any publishing professionals. These women not only worked for Lovinia's publisher, they'd worked directly with Lovinia.

"From his own pocket?" asked a fourth woman, a hollow-cheeked wisp of a girl who was so rail-thin she could be the poster child for Anorexia Anonymous. "Hard to imagine Pecker Boy has a generous cell in his body, given the slave wages he pays us."

Freckle Face snorted. "Obviously he's using corporate funds."

"Then why not have the company sponsor the scholarship?" asked Perky Blonde Number Two. "Why allow SARA to reap all that good publicity?"

"Too self-serving," said Freckle Face. "Sales of Lovinia's books will soar now that she's dead. Look at what happened after Prince died. Lovinia is to romance readers what Prince was to music lovers. It looks better if SARA, being a non-profit, takes the lead while we sit back and rake in the big bucks."

"Some of that money should go to us in the form of bonuses," said Botox Babe, "or hazard pay, given the crap we all put up with from her."

"Amen to that," said Perky Blonde Number One. "My blood pressure dropped back down into the normal range the moment I learned she'd died."

"I know what you mean," said Ms. Anorexia. "I haven't had an uninterrupted night's sleep in the two years I've been her line editor. That woman thought nothing of calling at three in the morning to yell at me. I'd lie awake afterwards, imagining all sorts of ways I could kill her and get away with it."

"I hope you tortured her first," said Freckle Face.

Ms. Anorexia chortled. "Now why didn't I think of that? Generally I'd just sneak up behind her and shove. She'd go flying—out a helicopter over the Hudson River, off the top of the Empire State Building, into the path of a speeding taxi—"

Or down a flight of stairs?

"—and splat! Bye-bye Lovinia."

Perhaps last night Ms. Anorexia had played out her fantasy. I made a mental note to mention her to Paisley as a possible suspect. Paisley might know her name and something more about her.

"Same here," said Perky Blonde Number Two. "We should definitely be compensated for all the harassment and bullying we suffered."

Freckle Face issued another snort. "Don't hold your breath about bonuses, girls. They'll probably use her death as an excuse for another round of layoffs."

I kept my head down but hung on every word as a waiter removed my half-eaten salad and another waiter placed the main course in front of me—overcooked conference chicken, limp green beans, and mushy pasta. Too bad the conference wasn't in Las Vegas. I would have placed a bet and cleaned up.

Once the wait-staff removed the main course and served dessert, the standard chocolate fudge cake always served with conference chicken, SARA's president made her way to the podium. She tapped the mic to gain everyone's attention. After a hush settled over the gathering, she said, "Before I introduce our keynote speaker, I have a few announcements."

I noted the pained expression on her face and wondered if it had anything to do with the membership response to the scholarship announcement. That decision had placed the entire Board on the collective caca list.

"For those of you who would like to pay your respects, Marcella Ford has informed me there will be a private viewing for

Lovinia Darling this evening for our membership from seven until nine. The address and directions to the funeral home are posted on the SARA conference app."

A negative murmur spread throughout the room and grew increasingly louder.

Botox Babe checked her phone and frowned. "We're also invited," she said.

"Like any of us would bother," said Perky Blonde Number Two.

"I couldn't stand dealing with her in real life," said Ms. Anorexia. "I'm certainly not going to waste any more time on her now that she's dead. Count me out."

The others agreed.

The SARA president tapped the mic again and waited for the rumble to cease. "I have several other announcements," she said, her voice filled with apology.

Once the room grew quiet again, she announced a few room changes for the afternoon workshops. Finally, she introduced the keynote speaker. "We all dream of seeing our books come to life on the silver screen. This year's keynote speaker is about to have that dream come true. By day she worked as a lowly assistant. At night she toiled to craft her novels. Last year *The Vampire Who Loved Me*, the first book in her five-book paranormal romance series, sold to Hollywood for two million dollars."

Audible gasps sounded throughout the audience.

"The first movie in the series releases next month. Let's hear a round of applause for this year's keynote speaker, Alyssa Bennigan."

As our speaker made her way to the lectern, I pulled the three books from my tote and noted that one of them was the first novel in her series. I flipped the book over and read the back cover copy. *A dystopian world populated by vampires and humans?* Hadn't that trope already been written to death?

"Who's in favor of blowing this gig and hopping over to the bar to toast our freedom from Lovinia?" asked Freckle Face.

They all agreed. Without so much as a nod goodbye to me, my tablemates pushed back their chairs, stood, and marched toward the nearest exit, leaving me alone at the table. Within minutes the wait-staff swooped in to clear their dishes.

I settled in to listen to Alyssa Bennigan, expecting to hear her secret to selling the movie rights to her books. However, it soon became apparent that her entire speech was nothing but crass self-promotion. A Power Point presentation, consisting mostly of selfies of her partying with Hollywood celebrities, accompanied her talk.

As she name-dropped, I realized Alyssa Bennigan, unlike most of the women in the ballroom, hadn't succeeded based on her talent. A Hollywood insider by virtue of her day job "in the business," she'd sold the rights to her books *after* she'd cut her Hollywood deal.

Sadly, I'd learned throughout my career that it's often not what you know but whom you know—or with whom you're sleeping. Our keynote speaker, with a face and body that qualified her as one of the "beautiful people," had rubbed more than elbows with quite a few extremely powerful people in SoCal, including the producer who handed her those big bucks for the rights to her series.

Alyssa Bennigan didn't directly come out and admit to having an affair with the guy, but she dropped enough hints that jumping to the conclusion was more of an itty-bitty baby step than an enormous leap. Apparently, her nights weren't entirely spent toiling over a keyboard.

One by one various authors began to leave the ballroom. I didn't for a minute believe they all needed a potty break at the same time, not when I noted the expressions on their faces or overheard some of their comments as they walked past me.

I stuck it out, hoping for some speck of advice. None came. Alyssa Bennigan ended her talk by saying, "We romance authors are a sisterhood. We need to support each other. You've all been given a copy of the first book in my series, thanks to the generosity of my publisher. Now you should purchase the other four books, and be sure to catch *The Vampire Who Loved Me* on its opening weekend to ensure huge box office receipts. Thank you!"

She blew a kiss, then strutted off the dais to tepid applause from the now half-empty room.

"Another Lovinia in the making?"

ELEVEN

I turned to find Paisley standing behind me. "She certainly has the attitude in spades."

"Not to mention the cluelessness." Paisley took note of the empty chairs around the table before settling into the seat next to me. "Were you all alone at lunch?"

"No, but I might as well have been." I told her about my rude tablemates. "Do you know any of them?"

"I know a few senior editors over there but none of the junior staff. Turnover in those positions is nearly as high as fast-food workers. People quickly move on to other houses, become agents, or leave publishing altogether after realizing it's not the glamorous career they imagined. Except for a handful of elite editors with megastar authors, most publishing professionals are extremely overworked and underpaid, especially those on the bottom rungs of the ladder."

"I had no idea."

"Neither do most starry-eyed college English majors."

So who profits in the world of publishing? From what I was learning, most authors couldn't live on what they made in royalties. Now Paisley claimed publishing didn't pay the majority of its employees very well, either. All those greenbacks from book sales had to be landing somewhere. My guess was into the bank accounts of greedy CEO's, corporate attorneys, and large shareholders. No wonder so many authors were turning to self-publishing.

How on earth did a business model like that survive? If the textile industry treated its designers the way publishing treated its authors and staff, we'd all be walking around in nothing but gunnysacks.

"Being ignored by those women did give me the opportunity to eavesdrop on their conversation, though, and I think I have another suspect for our list."

"The plot thickens. Spill, girl."

I told Paisley about Ms. Anorexia's murder fantasies.

She laughed. "You think Lovinia's line editor went crazy from sleep deprivation and killed her?"

"Maybe lack of sleep kept her from differentiating between fantasy and reality. She might not even realize she pushed Lovinia down those stairs."

The amused expression on Paisley's face shifted to one of pondering. "I suppose stranger things have happened."

"One problem, though. I don't know her name."

"I'll ask around."

"Natasha might know. Although I suppose it doesn't really matter. We wouldn't be using people's actual names, right?"

Paisley laughed. "Of course not."

"And we'll change things up considerably so no one from the

conference recognizes herself?"

"Relax, Gracie. We're writing fiction. Besides, I don't want anyone suing me."

"I hadn't thought about lawsuits."

"Then what's worrying you?"

"I'm not in the habit of destroying people's lives."

"And neither am I. Your tablemates were probably just blowing off steam. Who hasn't said she wished she could kill someone? We all utter statements like that from time to time, knowing we'd never act on them." She placed her hand over mine. "You have nothing to worry about."

I nodded as I heaved a sigh of relief. "By the way, we can cross Natasha off our list."

"You spoke with her?"

I explained what I'd learned about Natasha's finances and her arrangement with Lovinia.

Paisley pulled her legal pad from her tote bag and drew a line through Natasha's name. Then she added "line editor" with a question mark next to it. "I think she'd make a weak antagonist, though," she said. "We need a killer with a stronger motive."

"Have you learned anything?" I asked.

"Not really. This new memorial scholarship now dominates every conversation. Have you heard about it?"

"Hard not to. Are you going to the viewing?"

Paisley pulled a face. "Are you kidding? Give up a Saturday night in Manhattan to sit in a room with a dead body?"

"Maybe you and I should go."

She wrinkled her nose. "Why?"

"Doesn't the killer always show up at a viewing or funeral?"

"I think that's a cliché plot device used by mystery authors and

Hollywood screenwriters. Besides, a group of us have tickets to see *Hamilton* tonight."

"You were able to score tickets to the hottest show to hit Broadway in years?"

"We purchased them over a year ago. No way I'm not going. Not for anyone, let alone a dead Lovinia Darling. Have you seen the show yet?"

I frowned. "Lost my job, remember?" Once upon a time Blake and I attended the theater at least once a month, but we hadn't seen a show since I received my pink slip.

"Right. Sorry." She quickly turned the conversation back to the viewing. "Personally, I don't think anyone will bother to show up, given the dead body in question."

Maybe so, but I planned to attend, if for no other reason than to have another opportunity to strike up a conversation with Marcella Ford. However, I held back mentioning the possible DNA connection between Marcella and Lovinia.

Before releasing that speculative balloon, I needed to confirm Blake's hypothesis. If he was correct, I wanted to know the reason the two women had kept their relationship a secret. Any other course of action struck me as unethical.

Besides, my prying questions of SARA authors had already placed my big toe firmly over my personal comfort zone line. The last thing I wanted was to be labeled the source of an unfounded rumor based on similar eyes and ears. As much as I wanted a publishing contract, I couldn't sacrifice my integrity to achieve one.

Paisley tapped her pencil against the legal pad as she studied the list of suspects. "That leaves us with Penelope, Marcella, or Ronelle as our killer."

"Possible killer," I said. "We still don't know if we're dealing with a murder."

Paisley's head shot up, and she offered me a knowing smile. "Of course, we are."

"Not necessarily, according to the detective investigating Lovinia's death."

"He's not writing this book, Gracie."

I slapped my hand to my forehead. "Duh!" It didn't matter if Lovinia's death was ruled a murder or not. For the purposes of our collaboration, we needed to operate under the assumption that *someone* had pushed Lovinia down those stairs. The police findings didn't matter. Our "research" would establish our plot outline and our suspects' motives.

Paisley cocked her head. "Are we on the same page here?"

I nodded. "Fiction, not facts."

"Exactly." She returned to the list. "So given our three candidates, which one stands out to you as the most likely killer?"

I stared at the list and thought for a moment. "Until we know more about the history between Penelope and Lovinia, we really can't make a definitive decision about him."

"Agreed." Paisley wrote "motive?" next to Penelope's name. "So between Marcella and Ronelle?"

"We first need to find out if Ronelle was at the hotel last night. How do we do that?"

"I have an idea."

I raised both eyebrows.

Paisley pulled out her phone and began thumb-tapping across the keyboard. "Hyacinth has chaired the Cream of the Crop contest for the past five years. She has computer files containing the contact information of all the entrants."

"You think she'd give you Ronelle's phone number?"

"I don't see why not, especially if I tell her why I want it."

"And do what? Call to ask if she was in New York last night? Oh, and by the way, Ronelle, did you happen to push Lovinia Darling down a flight of stairs?"

Paisley's text swooshed its way into cyberspace. Then she raised her chin and said, "Really, Gracie, I'd be a bit more subtle than that."

"I certainly hope so! Speaking of subtle..." I nodded in the direction of the room behind us. Paisley and I were the only two authors still seated at any of the tables. All around us hotel staff were engaged in breaking down the room.

"I guess that's our cue to leave," said Paisley. She glanced at her watch. "I have an appointment with my publicist in a few minutes. I'll catch up with you later."

An appointment with my publicist. I wondered if I'd ever be able to utter those words. More than anything I wanted to be the next Paisley Prentiss and was so grateful she'd taken me under her wing.

We gathered up our belongings and departed the ballroom. Paisley headed down to the bar. I pulled out my conference schedule and checked the list of workshops currently in session.

~*~

Paisley and her group of friends weren't the only authors headed to the theater Saturday evening. SARA had arranged blocks of discounted tickets to a variety of plays and musicals for their members. By six o'clock spotting a romance author in the Crown Jewel was as likely as nabbing a ticket to *Hamilton*.

Consequently, Blake and I were on our own for dinner. We decided to head to The Lotus Blossom, one of our favorite restaurants in Chinatown. Tucked between an Asian market and a seafood wholesaler on Mulberry Street, the hidden gem boasted traditional red and gold wall coverings, black lacquer furnishings, white starched table linens, and some of the best Mandarin, Cantonese, and Szechuan food in the city.

Over steaming bowls of seafood soup I told him the second part of my good news.

"I don't get it, Gracie. It's one thing for Paisley to send your manuscript to her editor, but why would she want to collaborate on a book with you?"

"Because she loves the way I write and thought it would be a fun project."

"To co-author a novel with an unpublished author? That's rather unusual, isn't it?"

"James Patterson has done it for years."

Blake shook his head. "Patterson teams up with lesser-known *published* authors."

Really? Why didn't I know that? "I'll have you know, Blake, I'm not just an unpublished author; I'm a Cream of the Crop winner!"

"Yes, and I'm very proud of you, but what does Paisley get out of this partnership?"

"She said she's paying it forward."

"By introducing you to her agent and sending your manuscript to her editor. That I get, but this is entirely different. Has she pitched the idea for the book to her agent or editor?"

"Not yet. We're first figuring out a plot."

"A plot involving the murder of an unlikable romance author?"

"Exactly. Paisley got the idea after our breakfast this morning."

"And offered to partner with you? Why? Because you discovered Lovinia's body and have suspicions about her death?"

"Yes."

"Doesn't Paisley have deadlines for other books she has to write first?"

"Yes." I took a sip of my oolong tea before continuing. "That doesn't mean we can't work on this book at the same time. Unlike men, our lack of a Y chromosome enables women to juggle multiple projects at once."

Blake's face contorted into *The Look*. "Think about it. None of this makes sense, Gracie."

I stared at my husband. The man who should be over-the-moon thrilled for me was doing his best to burst my happiness balloon—just like when I told him about starting Relatively Speaking.

Only now, because he'd been proven right about my last venture, doubts began to creep into every crevice of my brain. Was Paisley as generous as I believed, or was I, as Blake inferred, the most naïve wannabe in the world of fiction writing? Was Paisley stringing me along? If so, why? What possible reason could she have?

None, I concluded. Some people are just genuinely nice human beings who generously give of themselves to others. Paisley Prentiss was one of those people. Blake was being his over-skeptical, overprotective self, doing his best to save me from myself when I needed no saving.

"You're wrong about Paisley," I said.

"Maybe I am. If so, I apologize in advance. However, you need to promise me one thing."

I took another sip of tea and eyed him over the rim of the cup. "What?"

"Before you immerse yourself in this project, have a contract drawn up between the two of you, outlining all responsibilities and how the advance and royalties will be split."

I grudgingly admitted he made sense. After spending decades in the textile industry, I knew better than to let emotion rule any business decisions. "I should have thought of that."

Blake had the good grace not to agree but added, "And I want our attorney to go over the contract before you sign on the dotted line."

I nodded.

We finished our soup in silence. While we waited for our entrée, I mulled over how to approach the topic of Lovinia's viewing.

As a writer, I should be able to pull the right words for any occasion from my brain, but on this occasion my gray matter failed me. While the waiter placed platters of Wor Shu Duck, fried rice, and steamed vegetables in front of us, I screwed up my courage and blurted out, "There's a viewing for Lovinia this evening, and I want to go to pay my respects."

"All right."

"You don't mind?"

"Why would I mind?"

"It's not exactly a fun Saturday evening activity."

"You discovered her body, Gracie. I think it's only appropriate that you attend the viewing."

Sometimes my husband totally surprises me. This was definitely one of those times.

Our dinner ended with orange slices and a fortune cookie for each of us. I broke mine open and pulled out the thin slip of paper. *A chance meeting opens doors to success and friendship.* I passed the fortune across the table to Blake. "See? This proves I'm right about

Paisley."

He read my fortune than handed me his. "Then what do you make of mine?"

His read: *Be on the lookout for coming events. They cast their shadows beforehand.*

I shrugged as I tossed the slip of paper onto the table. "Shadows aren't necessarily bad things, merely foreshadowing of things to come." *Right?*

TWELVE

After finishing dinner, Blake and I hopped on an uptown subway to attend Lovinia's viewing. Given her status in the publishing world, not to mention her legions of loyal fans, I expected to find Lovinia laid out at one of the Manhattan funeral homes of choice for deceased celebrities, dignitaries, and the Park Avenue elite.

Instead, Marcella had chosen a small memorial chapel on Tenth Avenue in Hell's Kitchen, not far from where I used to work in the Garment District. We arrived to find the sidewalk in front of the Eternal Peace Memorial Chapel devoid of mourning fans and without a single member of the press—tabloid or otherwise—in sight.

Even though this evening's viewing was a private affair reserved for SARA members and publishing professionals, in the age of Facebook, Twitter, Instagram, and flash mobs, how likely was it that word of Lovinia's death had not spread across the planet by now? I hadn't watched the morning news or looked at a newspaper all day, but surely today's edition of *The New York*

Times would have run an obituary, or at least a mention of her tragic and sudden death. After all, Lovinia Darling was a constant presence on their bestseller list.

Her fellow romance authors and everyone who worked with her might have loathed the woman, but the reading public knew nothing of the real Lovinia Darling. They worshipped her. So where were the scores of sobbing women clutching copies of Lovinia's books?

The street on either side of the chapel was empty except for a dog walker shepherding five designer pooches and a homeless man slumped on the steps of the building next door as he drank from a bottle wrapped in a brown paper bag. No makeshift memorial of flowers, candles, letters, signs, and teddy bears littered the sidewalk, indicating some of Lovinia's fans had previously shown up to pay homage to the Queen of Romance.

We climbed the half-dozen brownstone steps leading to a pair of well-worn mahogany double doors. A bell tinkled as Blake pulled open one of the doors. We stepped across the threshold into a dimly lit, somber foyer straight out of Charles Dickens. White veined black marble tile covered the floor. Dark oak paneling lined the walls from floor to ceiling. I glanced up at the sweeping staircase at the back of the foyer, half-expecting to find Miss Havisham, or at least her doppelganger, descending to greet us.

However, neither Miss Havisham nor anyone else appeared. An easel holding an ivory placard stood in the middle of the round claw-foot oak table that filled the center of the foyer. In the yellow light of a dusty crystal chandelier suspended above the table, I read the ornate calligraphy spelling out Lovinia's name. A decorative arrow below her name directed us to the room on the left.

Blake glanced down at the open guest book sitting in front of the placard. "Looks like we're the first visitors," he said.

"If what Paisley told me is correct, we may be the only visitors." I picked up the pen and wrote *Mr. and Mrs. Blake Elliott* on the first line of the first page. After setting the pen back on the table I slipped my hand into Blake's. Together we walked into the viewing room.

I expected to see Marcella at the viewing. After all, she'd organized it. However, I executed a double-take at the sight of Penelope McGregor sitting beside her. Given what I'd observed Friday and what Paisley had told me earlier in the day, he was one of the last people I'd ever expect to show up at Lovinia's viewing.

Although when I flashed back to the way I'd seen him comforting Marcella this morning, maybe I shouldn't have been so surprised. Perhaps he'd come more to support Marcella than pay his respects to the deceased.

Marcella rose to greet us. Her face with its red-rimmed, puffy eyes and tear-stained cheeks suggested a recent crying jag. She'd dressed all in black in a conservative suit, black stockings, and a pair of sensible black pumps that I pegged as Easy Spirit.

Standing before me, she took both of my hands in hers and offered me a sad smile. "Thank you for coming." Then she turned to Penelope, who had used his cane to leverage himself to his feet and huffed and puffed his way over to join us.

Penelope had forsaken his ubiquitous Stetson and traded in his blue jeans, suspenders, and plaid shirt for a conservative casual Friday white-collar outfit—a freshly pressed pair of Dockers, held up with a leather belt; a pale blue Oxford shirt; and a navy blazer. "This is Gracie Elliott," she said. "She discovered Lovinia's body in the stairwell."

Penelope studied me for a moment, as if trying to place me. I held my breath, hoping he wouldn't remember the first time he noticed me in the hotel lobby Friday afternoon. I didn't want to relive that embarrassing moment or be forced to offer an explanation for my outburst.

Then he said, "You won the Cream of the Crop Award, didn't you?"

I nodded and began breathing again. Marcella then turned questioningly to Blake. "And you are?"

"My husband Blake," I said. "He accompanied me to the conference."

Blake mumbled, "I'm sorry for your loss."

Marcella nodded. An awkward silence followed. Small talk has never been my forte, but someone had to keep the conversation going, and it didn't appear neither Marcella nor Penelope were so inclined. Therefore, even though I already knew the answer, I made a show of glancing around the room, then asked the obvious, "Where is everyone?"

Marcella shrugged. "It's Saturday night in Manhattan. Most of the authors already had dinner and theater plans." She sighed before adding somewhat reluctantly, "Besides, it's hardly a secret that there was no love lost between Lovinia and the SARA membership."

"Or her and anyone else," said Penelope, bitterness coloring his words.

"Including you?" I asked.

He scowled. "We had our differences."

"But still, you're here."

"For Marcella."

I turned back to Marcella. "You arranged for a private viewing, knowing no one would attend?"

"You came. And Penelope. Others still might show up." She shrugged again. "It seemed like the appropriate thing to do."

As I spoke with Marcella, I glanced at the closed casket behind her, puzzled by an invitation to a viewing where the deceased wasn't on view. I had hoped taking a look at a peaceful, reposing Lovinia would go a long way toward erasing the last image of her currently seared into my brain.

Instead, a framed photograph of a much younger Lovinia sat on top of the casket lid. If I'd had any doubts before about the relationship between Marcella and Lovinia, they immediately disappeared as my gaze shifted from the photo to the woman standing before me. The similarities were far more pronounced when comparing Marcella to the younger version of Lovinia.

"Will the settling of Lovinia's estate fall to you as her assistant?" I asked. After hearing Paisley talk about the daunting task of wading through a lifetime of her father's possessions, I could only imagine how much more difficult such a task would be for the person left to sort through the trappings of Lovinia's life.

Marcella's jaw dropped. "I...why would you ask such a personal question?"

"Forgive me. It's just that you seem to be the only person who was close to her, the only one who cared about her."

"She had no one else."

"Were the two of you related?"

For a fleeting moment an odd expression crossed Marcella's face. Fear? Anxiety? Apprehension? Before I could analyze the exact emotion, it disappeared, and Marcella quickly composed herself as she stepped closer to Penelope. "What would give you that idea?"

I nodded toward the photo. "I can't help but notice the strong resemblance."

Blake cleared his throat. I avoided looking at my husband because I knew beyond a shadow of a doubt that he was spearing me with *The Look*.

Marcella flushed a deep crimson and began to stammer. "I...we—" She turned to Penelope, her eyes pleading with him to bail her out of the conversation.

He shook his head. "There's no point keeping her secrets any longer. The old bat is dead."

Marcella's jaw dropped for a second time. "You can't let go even now? Really, Dad?"

Dad? Penelope McGregor was Marcella Ford's father?

My brain swam with questions, but before I could ask any of them, Penelope turned to me and said, "She was my ex-wife. Marcella is our daughter."

For a moment I could only stare alternately at the two of them while my brain processed that bombshell of a pronouncement. "Why the secrecy?"

"It's what Mother wanted," said Marcella, frowning at her father.

"And heaven forbid—" A coughing jag suddenly overtook Penelope. Marcella's expression turned from one of anger and annoyance at her father to one of concern. She placed her hand on his back while he took a hit from his nebulizer. Once the medicine calmed his lungs, he took a few calming breaths, then continued, "Heaven forbid anyone dare challenge the wishes of the Queen of Romance."

"But why hide the relationship?" I asked.

"Gracie..." Blake placed his hand on my shoulder, most likely as a warning to keep my nose out of Penelope and Marcella's business, but I ignored him as I waited for an answer to my question.

"We really don't need to go into that," said Marcella.

"What difference does it make now?" Penelope asked her. "She's dead. Maybe it's time the world learned the real story."

Before Marcella had a chance to protest further, Penelope turned to me and explained. "Many years ago my ex-wife's irresponsible actions resulted in the death of a young woman. Instead of taking responsibility, she orchestrated a cover-up."

"That's not true," said Marcella. "There was never any proof of her culpability in the woman's death and certainly not of a cover-up."

"Because she destroyed the evidence," said Penelope.

"I refuse to believe she'd do that."

"Believe what you want," said Penelope. "I know the truth."

"You weren't there. You can't know what really happened that night."

"I was married to her at the time, remember? You were a toddler. You have no idea what kind of life she led back then."

"She wasn't the monster you make her out to be," said Marcella.

Penelope stared down his nose at his daughter and raised both eyebrows. "Because she treated you so well?"

A pained expression settled over Marcella's face. She folded her arms around her torso and hung her head.

Penelope continued with his story. "She changed her name, walked away from her old life, and reinvented herself, even undergoing some plastic surgery to alter her looks."

Shades of Sidney Mandelbaum! "Drastic surgery?"

"Nothing major but enough to give her a slightly different appearance."

Apparently this came as news to Marcella, given her shocked expression. "You never told me—"

"I didn't see the point," said Penelope, "and I knew she wouldn't tell you."

I glanced over at the framed portrait on the coffin, then at Marcella with her receding chin that looked nothing like her father's squared jaw or her mother's tapered one. "A chin implant?"

Penelope nodded. "Along with a nose job and a sculpting of her cheekbones."

"And she immediately became a successful romance author?" I asked. From everything I'd heard about publishing over the last day and a half, I now knew how unusual that was. However, much had changed in the publishing world since Lovinia first broke onto the scene nearly forty years ago. Back then thousands of bookstores dotted the pre-Internet American landscape. Scores of publishing houses thrived, not yet gobbled up by a handful of huge conglomerates. Perhaps success came easier decades ago than it did now.

Penelope shook his head. "Success is often more about connections. My ex-wife knew people who were quite willing to roll out the red carpet for her in order to protect their own reputations and careers."

His implication stunned me. "Wait a minute. Are you suggesting Lovinia committed a crime and others were complicit in a cover-up? If you knew this, why didn't you go to the police?"

Marcella glared at her father. "Because none of it is true. Not a single word."

"What exactly did she do that led to the woman's death?" Had Lovinia embezzled money and placed the blame on someone else who then committed suicide? Did she cover up a hit-and-run? Commit a crime of passion? Whatever had happened must have been incredibly serious for her to go to such lengths. And what kind of connections could she have had that opened publishing's golden door for her?

"Mother said the woman died of natural causes. She had a bad heart. There's no huge conspiracy and never was. As for the plastic surgery, although I never knew about it, I'm not surprised, given her vanity."

Marcella pointed a finger at her father's chest. Her voice grew louder and angrier. "For years you've allowed your animosity toward Mother to compromise your logic. None of your accusations make any sense. They never have, and I can't believe you've brought all of this up again now that she's no longer here to refute you and defend herself, let alone that you'd air your stupid conspiracy theories in front of total strangers. It's nothing but nonsense!"

Before Penelope could respond, Blake placed his hand on my forearm and said, "This is really none of our business, Gracie. We're leaving."

"But—"

"Now, Gracie." He turned to Penelope and Marcella. "Again, we're very sorry for your loss."

Blake led me from the room, into the foyer, and toward the front door. "Wait," I said.

"You're not going back in there, Gracie."

"No, I have to pee. I'll never make it back to the hotel." I glanced around the dark foyer, finally noticing a small sign indicating restrooms off to the side of the staircase. I pointed to it. "I'll be right back."

Blake reluctantly released my hand. My husband knew better than to argue with the bladder of a woman who'd given birth to twins. "I'll wait right here for you."

Once inside the restroom, I pulled out my cell phone and shot off a quick text to Paisley: TOP SECRET! FOR YOUR EYES ONLY! Great plot twist: Penelope once married to Lovinia. Marcella their daughter. Will explain all tomorrow.

I held back mentioning Lovinia's possible involvement in some woman's death. For one thing, the topic was far too complicated for a text message. With Penelope and Marcella at odds over the facts, Lovinia might be totally innocent of any wrongdoing. More importantly, thanks to my husband, I had absolutely no details—not the woman's name, how she died, or where and when. With so little information, Lovinia might only be guilty of having been married to a man consumed by conspiracy theories and a hatred for his ex.

After taking care of business, I returned to Blake. Once on the sidewalk, I dug in my Fendi ash patent leather wedge sandals and confronted him. "I can't believe you did that!"

"Me? What about you? You were totally out of line, Gracie."

"But he was about to tell me—"

"It's none of our business. Besides, you have no idea how much of what he said is true. The guy harbors a huge grudge when it comes to his ex-wife."

Blake stepped into the street and raised his arm to hail a cab. As soon as one pulled to a stop at the curb, we settled into the back seat. "Where to?" asked the cabbie.

"Crown Jewel Hotel," said Blake.

I sat silently with my arms crossed over my chest. My husband placed his hand on my knee and said, "Stop pouting, Gracie. You know I'm right."

"I'm not pouting."

"Could have fooled me."

Of course Blake was right. He's always right—except when he's wrong—which doesn't happen very often. "Aren't you the least bit curious about the mystery surrounding Lovinia's past?"

Instead of answering me, he asked, "Do you want to know because you think it has something to do with her death?"

"I hardly think Penelope's suspicions have anything to do with Lovinia's death. She published her first book decades ago, back when my reading list consisted of *Yertle the Turtle* and *How the Grinch Stole Christmas*."

"Then it must be because of this book you and Paisley plan to write."

"What would be so wrong with that? Even if Penelope's suspicions are groundless, the plot potential is huge. But since you dragged me out before I had a chance to learn more, I'll never know. You may very well have kept me from having a bestseller, Blake Elliott."

"You're writing fiction, Gracie, not true crime. Make something up."

"I'd still like to know what Lovinia did that makes Penelope suspect she killed that woman."

Blake tightened his lips and shook his head as he filled his lungs with air. I knew he was most likely silently counting to ten or twenty or two hundred. Finally he exhaled and said, "Didn't you see that your prying was making Marcella extremely uncomfortable? It's not like you to put your own selfish reasons before a woman suffering over the loss of her mother."

That made me squirm in my seat. I unfolded my arms and sighed. Once more my husband was right. "I was very insensitive, wasn't I?"

"Extremely."

"I should go back to apologize." I leaned forward, about to knock on the Plexiglas partition separating us from the driver.

Blake reached for my hand and withdrew it, placing it back on my lap. "Nice try, Gracie. Write her a letter."

I scowled at him. "Are you accusing me of having ulterior motives?"

"I think I don't want to give you the opportunity of proving me right."

I bit my tongue. Hard. At times like this, discretion was definitely the better part of valor. Besides, at that moment my cell phone dinged to alert me to a text. I pulled the phone from my Fendi clutch bag.

"Who's texting you on a Saturday night?" asked Blake. He leaned over in an effort to glimpse the message.

"Paisley."

"Your partner in crime?"

"Crime-*writing!*"

"Of course. I thought you said she had tickets for the theater tonight."

I glanced at the time on my phone. "The curtain doesn't go up for another ten minutes."

"What's so important that it couldn't wait until morning?"

I read the text, keeping the phone turned away from Blake's prying eyes: Wow! Never saw that coming. More news. Found our killer. Lots to talk about. Breakfast 6:30. Meet in lobby.

THIRTEEN

Six-thirty? On a Sunday morning? Whatever Paisley had to tell me must be pretty important if it couldn't wait a few extra hours, especially since she probably wouldn't get to bed much before midnight.

Then again, I had no idea where she lived. She probably had to leave the conference early in order to catch a flight home.

I pondered her message, wondering what she'd meant by "found our killer." That Lovinia really had been murdered and she knew the killer's identity? Or had she simply come up with the perfect perpetrator for our book?

Either way, I didn't want to discuss this news with Blake. Although I wasn't in the habit of lying to my husband, nothing good would come of answering truthfully right now.

Without responding to the text, I turned off my phone and dropped it back inside my clutch. "She's just bored and killing time before the show starts."

I sensed Blake staring at me but refused to make eye contact with him. Knowing my husband well enough to know he knew I was hiding something, I stared out the window and pretended otherwise.

"What would you like to do the rest of the evening?" he asked once we arrived back at the Crown Jewel.

I glanced at my watch. It wasn't even eight-thirty. The last thing I wanted was to spend any more time than necessary in our depressing, germ-infested, throwback-to-the-seventies hotel room. "You have any suggestions?"

"How about a walk?"

I held out my hand. With fingers entwined, Blake and I headed west toward Madison Ave. However, I should have known that window-shopping on a street with some of the priciest shops in the world would only pour salt on my wounded, unemployed ego.

We'd strolled about half a mile when the temperature suddenly plummeted, and the warm breeze that had made for a perfect spring evening stroll kicked up into a chilly, fierce wind. We raced back to the hotel, ducking into the lobby just as the first heavy drops of rain hit the pavement.

"So much for that," said Blake. "How about a drink in the bar?"

I'd consumed enough alcohol last night for the next three months. "Margarita and I have had a falling out. I'll just take my insensitive self upstairs to our room and hunker down with the microbes. Maybe I'll fire up my laptop and start my next book."

"Not still sulking, are you, Gracie?"

"Me? Perish the thought!"

Blake speared me with *The Look*. Yes, I was still sulking. He knew it, and he knew that I knew he knew. That's what happens when you're married for nearly a quarter of a century.

Still, in the name of peace, harmony, and a continuing marriage, I sucked up my sulk and forced a smile, hoping it appeared genuine. Did he buy it? Probably not. But in the name of peace, harmony, and a continuing marriage, he smiled back. Détente. You've got to love it!

Back in Mid-Century Microbe Central, we both settled into bed. Side-by-side, laptops propped on our knees, we spent the next several hours pecking away at our keyboards, Blake on his cultural opus, while I pretended to work on my next book. In reality I was surfing the 'net.

Penelope's bombshell about Lovinia's earlier life had piqued my curiosity. Exactly what had she done that Penelope believed led to a woman's death and the subsequent creation of a new identity?

I began by searching "Lovinia Darling." Google offered up several thousand sites, but a quick scan of the first few pages of URLs convinced me I needed to narrow my search parameters.

I next tried "Lovinia Darling early life," then "Lovinia Darling past." Both provided nothing but official biographies that omitted any references to her early years other than having grown up in a home filled with books and that she learned to read before her third birthday.

"Lovinia Darling's real name" produced considerable speculation that she wrote under a pseudonym. Most of her fans doubted any parent would pair that particular first name with the surname Darling. Clearly those comments were written before Kim Kardashian and Kanye West produced bouncing baby North West.

I then ran a search of "author secret identity" and "author secret pen name." Some interesting facts popped up, including one current literary bestseller whose real identity has become a viral guessing-game, but not a single mention of Lovinia.

Finally, I searched "author dark past" and found an absolute shocker, only not about Lovinia. I learned that a very famous English mystery author had gone to prison for helping kill her friend's mother back in the nineteen-fifties in New Zealand when the girls were teenagers.

I glanced over at Blake, itching to discuss the case with him but thought better of it, having led him to believe I was working on a new book. I suppose I could say I stumbled upon the information while researching an idea for the new book, but how would I spin such research around a romantic comedy plot? He'd see right through me, and we'd had enough of that for one evening.

Instead I powered down my computer.

"Calling it a night?" he asked.

I nodded. "You can keep working if you want."

He gave me a look, but not *The Look*. This particular look involved a sheepish grin and a wiggling of eyebrows that left no room for interpretation.

~*~

Before going to bed last night I had set the alarm on my phone for six o'clock, but I woke before it went off—way before. Blake opened one eye, glanced at the bedside clock that read five-fifteen, and groaned. "Why are you up so early?"

"I was invited to a breakfast."

"At this hour?"

"I couldn't sleep. The breakfast is scheduled for six-thirty."

"You didn't mention a breakfast yesterday."

"Didn't I? Go back to sleep. I'll see you in a few hours."

He pulled the blanket over his head as he muttered something indiscernible. A minute later his snores filled the room.

After taking a long, steamy shower, I dressed to the accompaniment of more snores, pairing white linen slacks with a gray silk T-shirt, charcoal raw silk blazer, and a pair of black leather Giuseppe Zanotti stacked heel platform sandals. I accessorized with a silver and black trellis patterned silk scarf I'd designed several years ago and a pair of silver hoop earrings.

I still had forty minutes before my scheduled meeting with Paisley. Instead of sitting in the darkened room, I stuffed one of the many freebie books I'd received over the weekend into my conference tote and headed down the hall to the elevator, planning to read in the lobby until Paisley arrived.

However, when the elevator doors slid open, I was surprised to find Paisley standing in the middle of the lobby. She wasn't alone. Hyacinth stood chatting beside her.

I had assumed Paisley and I were having a private breakfast meeting. A twinge of guilt twisted my insides. What if Paisley had ignored me and spilled the top-secret beans from my text of last night? Although Penelope professed not to care who knew about Lovinia's past, Marcella, for reasons not made clear to me, wanted to keep the past buried.

From what I'd observed of Hyacinth, the woman thrived on gossip. Now thanks to my big mouth—or more accurately, my speedy texting fingers—the entire SARA membership might soon learn of the familial relationship between Penelope, Marcella, and Lovinia.

Blake was right—as usual. Maybe I needed to sign up for sensitivity training. But first I faced the looming prospect of major damage control, if that was even possible at this point. Who knew how many people Paisley had already blabbed to about Lovinia?

And how many of those people had already blabbed to others?

Paisley spied me walking toward them across the nearly empty lobby and said something to Hyacinth. Both women turned to face me, waiting silently for me to join them.

Once again I'd overdressed. Paisley wore a pair of black jeans and a white short-sleeve scoop neck T-shirt. Hyacinth had dressed in a pair of lavender jeans and a bright purple short-sleeve T-shirt. Neon green glitter lettering that read *Romance Writers Have Great Climaxes* filled her ample chest. I stifled a groan. Hopefully Blake wouldn't cross paths with her today.

Once I came toe-to-toe with them, Paisley linked her arm through mine. "Well, you certainly dropped a bombshell last night. How did you ever manage to find out that Penelope was married to Lovinia and Marcella is their daughter?"

Hyacinth didn't bat an eyelash, confirming my theory that she already knew. I quickly scanned the immediate vicinity. Satisfied that the few other people up this early and in the lobby were out of earshot, I asked, "Who else have you told?"

"Just Hyacinth," said Paisley.

I turned to Hyacinth. "Please keep this news to yourself for now."

"Why? It's such juicy gossip!"

So much for damage control. Everyone at the conference would know by the start of the first workshop this morning. I tried a different approach. "I don't think it's fair to Marcella. She's dealing with the loss of her mother. You should have some compassion."

Hyacinth quirked her head and skewed her mouth, considering my words. Without saying anything, she linked her arm through my free one, and the two of them led me toward the hotel restaurant. "Why don't we go to the coffee shop?" I suggested.

"This will be more private," said Paisley. "We have lots to discuss."

At this early hour I doubted we'd find many people at the coffee shop, let alone other authors, but short of tackling them both, I had no option other than allowing myself to be dragged into the pricey restaurant.

Paisley led us to a table toward the back of the restaurant. As soon as we had taken our seats a waiter handed us menus and poured coffee. "We also have a full breakfast buffet available this morning," he said. "It will be available in about ten minutes."

Once he left, Hyacinth said, "Sugar, you are a woman of exceptional talents. We've known Penelope for years and never had a clue. You waltz in for the weekend and manage to uncover the secret to end all secrets. I am thoroughly impressed."

"How did you do it?" asked Paisley.

Instead of answering her, I said, "I wish you hadn't told anyone, Paisley. Marcella was extremely upset that Penelope spilled the family beans."

Paisley shrugged. "What difference does it make? Lovinia is dead."

"That's what Penelope said, but for some reason it matters to Marcella."

"That woman needs a good therapist," said Paisley. "She's probably suffering from some form of Stockholm Syndrome, given the way Lovinia treated her."

"I don't see why it should matter to her," said Hyacinth, "unless there are other deep dark secrets she doesn't want the world to know about Lovinia."

There were, but I decided I'd done enough damage and wouldn't divulge Penelope's assertion that Lovinia was responsible for a woman's death. I had neither proof nor details. If Penelope wanted to besmirch his ex-wife's reputation further, that was between him and his daughter. I couldn't sweep up the beans I'd already spilled, but I could hold fast to the ones I hadn't.

"Did you dig up any other dirt on Lovinia?" asked Hyacinth.

I decided to play dumb. "Dirt?"

"Did you learn any more deep dark secrets about her?"

"No." I shook my head for emphasis. "That was all I learned. I doubt there's more."

Hyacinth cocked her head and offered me a catbird smile. "There's always more, sugar."

Paisley waved her hand dismissively. "Gracie is probably right. I'm sure Marcella is Lovinia's sole beneficiary. She's protecting her inheritance. All those royalties will now go to her. She just wants to make sure Lovinia's books continue to sell for years to come."

I hadn't thought about that. Marcella would prevail upon her father to keep mum in order to protect the brand that was Lovinia Darling. However, given what I'd learned last night while surfing the 'net, maybe rumors about Lovinia's past would have no impact at all on sales of her books. After all, the author who helped kill her friend's mother decades ago still continually made the bestseller lists.

Hyacinth had an opposing theory. "Learning that Lovinia led everyone to believe Marcella was nothing more than an assistant might anger some readers enough to boycott her books," she said, "especially if the tabloids get hold of the story."

"I hardly think a few readers deciding not to buy another Lovinia Darling book will have much impact on Marcella's future income," I said. I told them about the English author.

"Times have changed," said Paisley. "That news came out decades prior to Twitter, Facebook, and Instagram. Nowadays we see careers destroyed by readers who take offense to some offhand remark an author makes on social media. The next thing you know, a difference of opinion spins out of control and goes viral. A media savvy author avoids all controversial topics."

"Not to mention any whiff of impropriety or scandal," added Hyacinth, "unless, of course, she's writing a nonfiction tell-all book. Then she'd encourage controversy as a way of selling more books."

"Isn't the whole point of social media to interact with your readers?" I asked.

"Chat with readers as much as you want," said Paisley, "but keep your personal life separate from your author life. For instance, I never discuss politics, religion, or anything controversial on social media. I don't want to alienate any readers." She offered me a wink and a grin before adding, "Liberal, conservative, moderate, or anarchist, I want them all to buy my books."

I maintained a very limited presence on social media, mostly using it to keep up with out-of-town relatives too busy or too lazy to pick up a telephone every few months. I could count my social media "friends" on both hands and have fingers left over. However, I'd learned most publishers not only expected their authors to interact with readers on social media, some even demanded it.

The waiter returned to take our orders. Both Paisley and Hyacinth opted for menu items, probably after checking the fifty-dollar price of the buffet. Paisley decided on a Western omelet with a side of breakfast sausage. Hyacinth ordered French toast topped with sliced bananas and wet pecans along with a side of scrambled eggs and Canadian bacon.

Not only had my eyes bugged out over the cost of the buffet, I cringed at the prices of the à la carte items. "I'll just have a cup of coffee," I said.

"Don't be ridiculous," said Paisley. "Order breakfast."

I started to protest, but she stopped me midsentence. "My treat. Consider it a reward for your amazing undercover work."

"Only if you allow me to leave the tip," I said, feeling uncomfortable over Paisley's constant generosity.

"Absolutely not," she said. "Order something, or I'll order for you."

Reluctantly I ordered the cheapest item on the menu, a sixteen-dollar Continental breakfast that consisted of a glass of fresh-squeezed orange juice, a basket of assorted breads and muffins, and a fresh fruit salad.

Once the waiter left, I thanked Paisley, then quickly changed the subject. "What did you mean last night when you texted that you'd found the killer? Do you have proof Lovinia was really murdered?"

"Not exactly," said Paisley, "but I'm sure Detective Vanslootenberger—"

"You spoke with him?"

"I called him as soon as Hyacinth and I figured out what most likely happened to Lovinia."

"How did you know whom to call?"

Paisley looked puzzled. "What do you mean?"

"I don't recall mentioning his name to anyone. I've had trouble remembering it. That's why I keep referring to him mostly as 'the detective.'"

Paisley laughed. "It is an odd name, isn't it? But I've always been good with names, especially unusual ones. Anyway, I called the NYPD and asked to speak with the detective who investigated the Friday night death at the Crown Jewel Hotel. He called me back within five minutes. He's probably wringing a confession out of our killer as we speak."

"If he hasn't already," added Hyacinth. "For all we know, she's behind bars."

My head spun—literally and figuratively as I focused back and forth between Paisley and Hyacinth while processing this sudden twist. "*She?* Which she? What do you think happened?"

"After Paisley told me about the suspects list the two of you had generated, I called Ronelle Crenshaw last night before going to dinner," said Hyacinth. "Her husband told me she's in New York on business."

"Hyacinth unleashed her considerable Southern charms on him," said Paisley, offering a congratulatory pat to Hyacinth's shoulder. "She quickly learned the 'business' was a legal matter."

"And bless his heart," said Hyacinth, "when I mentioned that I was also in New York for the weekend and would love to see her, quick as a Blue Ridge possum he told me she's staying directly across the street from us at the Radisson Hotel. Even gave me her room number."

"That doesn't mean she killed Lovinia," I said, "even if she did come to New York to watch her served with the subpoena."

Paisley poured cream into her cup, then took a sip of her coffee. Still holding the cup near her mouth, she said, "No, but at the least it makes her a person of interest in the eyes of the police and might connect a few dots."

"Only if Lovinia's death is ruled a homicide," I reminded her. "Remember, Detective Vanwhatshisname led me to believe they have no evidence to indicate anything had occurred other than a tragic accident."

Paisley grinned. "That was before I told him about the lawsuit Ronelle filed and Lovinia's reaction to the subpoena."

Which Detective Vanwhatshisname already knew from questioning me Friday night, but at the time I hadn't known the name of the person who filed the lawsuit or that she had booked a room across the street from the Crown Jewel. "So now he thinks Lovinia *was* murdered? Based on Ronelle being in New York?"

The waiter arrived with our food, and Paisley held off answering until he'd placed the platters in front of us. After he headed back in the direction of the kitchen, she continued. "He said it's all circumstantial evidence, but he'd check into it."

"However, if Ronelle did kill Lovinia," said Hyacinth, pouring half a bottle of maple syrup onto not only her French toast but her scrambled eggs and sausage, "she'd certainly crack under questioning. It's not like she's a CIA operative or Navy SEAL or anything."

"What does she do for a living?" I asked.

"She teaches kindergarten."

I leaned back against my chair and tried to make sense of all this. Paisley and I had allowed our imaginations to run wild, but now it appeared our fictional musings might not be so fictional after all. "Talk about truth being stranger than fiction! Do you really think a kindergarten teacher is capable of murder?"

"Given the right circumstances?" asked Paisley. "Anyone is capable of anything. It's really too bad you didn't get a glimpse of her Friday night when Lovinia came crashing through the door."

"You didn't, did you?" asked Hyacinth, speaking around an enormous mouthful of French toast.

I shook my head. "No, and believe me, I've searched every cell in my brain, hoping that some telltale memory lurked hidden in a deep crevice. I can't remember seeing or hearing anyone other than the door slamming open and Lovinia plummeting toward me. It all happened so quickly."

Hyacinth shook her head, clicked her tongue against the roof of her mouth, and said, "Damn shame."

FOURTEEN

I'm no expert on police procedures, but if events unfolded as Paisley and Hyacinth speculated, with Ronelle Crenshaw breaking under the pressure of questioning and admitting her guilt, I had just cracked my second murder investigation—with a little help from my new author friends, of course. I always give credit where credit is due.

I nibbled on a triangle of buttered whole-wheat toast as I thought about how best to explain this turn of events to Blake. He wouldn't be happy, but unlike my previous investigation into the murder of Sidney Mandelbaum, at least this time I hadn't placed myself in danger—except for nearly being flattened by Lovinia's plummeting body, but he could hardly blame me for that!

"What's spinning around in that brilliant brain of yours, sugar?"

Hyacinth's question snapped me out of my thoughts and back into the here-and-now. She and Paisley stared at me from across the table. "If Ronelle killed Lovinia," I said. "I'm two for two when it comes to crime-solving. Maybe I've missed my calling."

"What do you mean?" asked Paisley, a forkful of omelet paused midway between her plate and her mouth. "You planning to switch from romance to mystery writing?"

"No, my heart is firmly planted in the romance genre, whether it's romantic comedy or collaborating with you on a romantic suspense. I'll always need my hero and heroine and that happily-ever-after ending."

She nodded. "I sense a 'but', though."

"More a 'however' than a 'but'," I said.

"Meaning?" asked Hyacinth.

"From what I've learned this weekend, making significant money as a romance author is about as likely as the Kardashians joining a convent. If Blake and I are to have a retirement that affords us a comfortable lifestyle, I need to replace the income I lost when the textile industry outsourced my design career to a third-world nation."

"I'm not following you," said Hyacinth. "What does that have to do with Ronelle killing Lovinia?"

"I'm thinking maybe I should get licensed as a private investigator and hang out a shingle."

Paisley's eyebrows shot up, and she nearly choked on a mouthful of egg. She reached for her water and after taking a few gulps asked, "Are you serious?"

"Why not? If Ronelle did kill Lovinia, you and I helped break the case."

"I think there's more to becoming a P.I. than a bit of author brainstorming," she said.

"I suppose. For one thing, I'd probably have to learn to shoot a gun, and I'm not all that comfortable with the idea of carrying a loaded firearm on my hip or in my purse."

"A smart woman is an armed woman," said Hyacinth. "My daddy taught me to shoot when I was no more than knee-high to a grasshopper."

I pointed to my chest. "This woman is smart enough to know she's a perpetual klutz and a disaster waiting to happen. Chances are I'd shoot myself by accident."

"Then maybe you shouldn't consider the idea," said Paisley.

"You're probably right," I said. "Besides, Blake might kill me. He exercised Herculean restraint when I opened Relatively Speaking."

Hyacinth had shoveled a large forkful of French toast into her mouth. Once she washed the food down with a swig of coffee and wiped a dribble of maple syrup from her chin, she asked. "What's Relatively Speaking?"

"My failed entrepreneurial venture into senior citizen matchmaking."

She laughed. "Well, sugar, if he kills you, you can investigate your own murder."

"That would certainly put a new twist on paranormal investigations," said Paisley. "Maybe you should consider writing a romantic mystery series about a ghost who solves murders, beginning with your—I mean, her—own." She thought about that for a moment before adding, "Although I don't see how you'd manage a happily-ever-after ending when your heroine is a ghost."

"Can ghosts even have romances?" asked Hyacinth.

"I'll ask the next time I encounter one," I said.

The shift in conversation reminded me of another topic I wanted to discuss. "Speaking of writing," I said. "Where do we go from here on our collaboration, Paisley? Whether Ronelle has an alibi or not, she'd make a great killer for our book."

"I was thinking the same thing," said Paisley. "I've got that deadline looming in a few weeks, and as you know, I'm nowhere near ready to turn the manuscript in to my editor. Why don't you start working up a synopsis and the first few chapters? Send them to me when you're finished. As soon as I put my latest baby to bed, we can figure out a schedule for how our collaboration will work."

I hesitated for a moment, trying to find a diplomatic way to present my husband's demand for a signed legal document without offending her. When nothing sprang to mind, I had no recourse but to take the blunt road. "Blake said we should sign a contract first."

Paisley smiled. "Of course he did. He wants to make sure I don't take advantage of you."

"Not that you ever would," said Hyacinth. She patted Paisley's hand. "You're far too honest." Hyacinth then turned to me. "You have no idea how lucky you are to have Paisley Prentiss in your corner, Gracie. Many unpublished authors would kill for such an opportunity." Her cheeks flushed scarlet as she realized what she'd said and quickly added, "Figuratively speaking, of course."

Good grief! I didn't want Paisley to think I was suspicious of her motives. Blake was too overprotective sometimes, but he was also right. This was a business partnership and needed the structure of a contract to protect both parties. "Believe me, I'm truly grateful, and I certainly don't think—"

Paisley held up her hand. "I understand, Gracie. We're entering into a business agreement, and everything should be spelled out in writing. My agent has already suggested we do that. Tell your husband not to worry. Drawing up a contract will be Item Number One on our to-do list."

We continued with our meals until Hyacinth glanced at her watch and gasped. "Look at the time! We've got to scoot, Paisley." She quickly shoveled the remainder of her breakfast into her mouth and drained her coffee cup.

"Is there a workshop starting this early?" I asked. According to the schedule, the first morning workshop didn't begin until nine o'clock. I checked my own watch. It read seven-forty.

"We have a committee meeting beginning in five minutes," said Paisley, pushing back from the table. "Take your time, Gracie. I'll sign for the breakfast on my way out. We'll catch up with you later."

That explained why Paisley had wanted to meet so early. With nowhere to go for over an hour and not wanting to disturb Blake if he still slept, I lingered over my coffee and nibbled at a blueberry muffin while I checked my email. I was busy deleting spam messages when a familiar gravely baritone said, "Good morning, Mrs. Elliott. May I join you?"

I looked up to find Penelope McIntosh, once again dressed in his cowboy attire, standing in front of me. "Of course. I'd love the company." Especially this particular company. Perhaps minus Marcella at his side, Penelope would continue his tale of Lovinia's earlier life and fill in some of the missing puzzle pieces.

He scoped out the table with the remains of Hyacinth and Paisley's breakfasts. "You're sure I'm not intruding?"

I dropped my phone back into my messenger bag. "No, my breakfast companions needed to dash off to a meeting."

"Very well." He pulled out the chair directly across from me and slowly lowered himself into the seat, hooking his cane onto the back of the chair next to him. He then removed his ten-gallon hat and placed it on the chair's seat.

A busboy immediately appeared to clear the dirty dishes and place a fresh table setting in front of Penelope. A waiter followed behind with a pot of coffee and a menu, but Penelope waved the menu away. "I'll have coffee, a large orange juice, three eggs scrambled hard, a double order of bacon, home fries, and buttered rye toast."

I sipped my coffee while the waiter filled Penelope's coffee cup. Once he turned back toward the kitchen and was out of earshot, I said, "I'm glad we've run into each other. I want to apologize for being overly nosey last night. My curiosity often gets the better of me, and I'm afraid I may have opened some old wounds."

Penelope shook his head. "If you mean Marcella's reaction, those wounds have never healed. They've festered her entire life. Sometimes I think she revels in playing the role of the martyred daughter."

I had to agree with Paisley's earlier assessment of Marcella. From everything I'd observed, a good therapist would do wonders for Marcella. I itched to say so but quashed the urge. Instead I said, "I imagine it wasn't easy growing up in Lovinia's shadow."

"All Marcella has ever wanted was her mother's love and approval, two things my ex-wife was incapable of giving anyone, but Marcella never stopped hoping her mother would one day love and admire her."

"Is that why the two of you divorced? Because Lovinia was incapable of caring about anyone other than herself?"

Penelope stared at me for a moment. Was he debating whether or not to explain more or tell me to mind my own business? His expression gave no clue. Finally he said, "That along with other things."

"Last night you claimed she was responsible for a woman's

death. Is that true?"

He heaved a sigh as he nodded once. "In my opinion, yes."

"But opinion isn't fact, and Marcella doesn't agree with you."

Penelope's features hardened, and his voice took on a bitter edge. "Marcella was little more than a baby at the time. She remembers nothing of that period in her life and only knows the lies her mother continually fed her."

"What are the facts?"

Penelope opened his mouth to speak, but at that moment the waiter appeared with his breakfast, obviously dished out from the buffet bar at the center of the restaurant. No way that meal was cooked to order so quickly. Once the artery-clogging breakfast was placed in front of him, the waiter topped off our coffees before leaving.

Penelope shoveled several forkfuls of egg and potatoes into his mouth. Then he picked up a slice of bacon and chewed on one end of it as he answered my question. "Cocaine happened. The recreational drug of choice back in the late seventies."

I'd seen enough movies over the years to know something about the drug scene in New York during that decade when the snorting of white powder proliferated among the Young Turks of Wall Street and within the celebrity-filled party atmosphere of Studio 54 and other clubs. "Was Lovinia a stockbroker?"

Penelope shook his head. "She was a senior editor at..." He hesitated. "...at a major New York publishing house."

"Is that how the two of you met?"

He shoveled more food into his mouth and nodded. "Three years earlier. She was an editorial assistant at the time."

A very ambitious one, no doubt. I might not know much about the publishing industry, but I did know there were quite a few positions between editorial assistant and senior editor. However, I kept the comment to myself. "How does the New York drug scene back in the seventies connect Lovinia to a woman's death? Was it a DUI?"

"No." He polished off his second cup of coffee before continuing. "She brought nose candy to the office as her contribution to the staff Christmas party. At some point her assistant slumped onto a table, but no one paid any attention to her, probably because everyone else was busy getting high. She lay there for hours before someone realized she was dead."

"From an overdose?"

"That's my guess."

"Was Lovinia charged?"

"No one was charged. The staff scurried around flushing evidence down the toilets and cleaning up all traces of white powder before calling for an ambulance."

"Wasn't an autopsy performed?"

Penelope shook his head. "My ex-wife told the paramedics her assistant suffered from an underlying heart condition."

"Did she?"

He shrugged. "Possibly. All I know is the death was ruled cardiac arrest from natural causes, and no one ever investigated what really happened that night."

Did the woman die from an overdose, or did she suffer a heart attack without ever having snorted any cocaine? Could her life have been saved if someone at the party had noticed her collapse and immediately called an ambulance? "Doesn't that seem unusual?"

"Maybe by today's standards, but keep in mind this all happened nearly forty years ago when violent crime ran rampant in New York City. The police and hospitals were stretched to their limits. If nothing seemed suspicious, no one looked too closely. Slap on a toe tag and move to the next body."

"Were you at that party?"

"I was home babysitting Marcella, as I was most nights while my ex-wife was out partying. Wall Street stockbrokers weren't the only ones into coke back then. The drug was pervasive among all sorts of professionals—actors, bankers, editors, agents, even doctors. I've often suspected an autopsy wasn't performed because the doctor was covering his own ass."

"What do you mean?"

"If he recognized the dead woman from one of the clubs he frequented, an investigation into her death might reveal things about his own life he'd rather keep hidden."

Talk about a multi-tiered conspiracy theory! Perhaps Marcella was right about her father. "You're making some wild accusations."

He shrugged away my suggestion. "Not really. You had to have lived here back then."

"But you don't even know if the woman used cocaine before she collapsed."

"If you were a young professional in the late seventies in New York City, you were probably doing coke at least occasionally."

Still, that didn't prove anything about the cause of the woman's death. "Present company included?"

He nodded. "Only up until Marcella came along. Someone had to take responsibility for the baby. My ex-wife certainly didn't."

I heard the bitterness in his voice and wondered if it was over Lovinia's behavior or him having to give up the party scene. Penelope McIntosh certainly didn't strike me as the party animal type, but for all I knew he might have been a real swinger back in the seventies. People change. Some grow old and fat; others mature and gain wisdom with age. Some do both.

"If the people at the office party destroyed all evidence of the cocaine," I asked, "what precipitated Lovinia's change of career and identity?"

"Her co-workers began to whisper. They'd cast sideways glances at her. Conversations would abruptly end when she entered a room." He grew silent for a moment, then added, "Or maybe none of this happened, and it was all a manifestation of her increasing paranoia."

He shoved another strip of bacon into his mouth. "She was doing a lot of coke by then and failing to meet deadlines. Eventually, she lost her job."

"Yet she was able to write publishable novels as a coke addict?"

"Not until after she OD'd a few months later. She agreed to go into rehab to avoid prosecution for drug possession. Once she'd cleaned up, she began writing."

"And she stayed clean?"

"Scared straight, thanks to that near-death experience. Six months later she'd completed her first novel and had no qualms about blackmailing her former boss into buying the book."

My mouth dropped open. "How in the world did she manage that?"

"They bought their stash from the same supplier. She threatened to spill the beans on him if he didn't start publishing her."

"Had he even seen the manuscript at that point? What if she couldn't write her way out of a paper bag?"

Penelope shrugged. "I suppose he would have hired someone

to rewrite the book. She had him by the *cojones*. Luckily for him, after years of editing romance, she knew exactly how to craft a saleable one."

When she wasn't plagiarizing other authors or relying on someone else to write her books for her. I wondered if Penelope knew that Marcella had hired a ghostwriter for her mother.

"She then legally changed her name and her looks," he said, "creating the persona of Lovinia Darling."

"Lovinia Darling is a pen name?"

"Of course."

"Why not just write under her new name?"

"A pen name added another layer of separation between her old life and her new one. Legal name changes are public record. She didn't want anyone digging around and stumbling upon her past."

This explained why I failed to find anything about the "old" Lovinia when I searched the Internet last night. "I'm assuming for this reason she chose an extremely common name? Something like Mary Johnson or Patricia Miller?"

Penelope nodded. "Something like that."

"And what about you?" I asked.

"What about me?"

"What was your role in this new life she created?"

"By then I'd had enough and filed for divorce."

"Did you sue for custody of Marcella?"

Penelope began to wheeze and reached for his nebulizer. After taking a puff, he continued. "I tried to get custody of Marcella. However, my ex-wife's lack of maternal instincts ran a distant second to her capacity for vindictiveness. Even though she couldn't have cared less about being a mother to Marcella, she fought me for custody. Back then the courts almost always sided with the mother, no matter her past history. All she had to do was prove she'd completed rehab and was no longer using drugs."

"Even though she was responsible for her assistant's death?"

"I had no way of proving that." Penelope shoveled more of his breakfast into his mouth. "So have I sated your curiosity, Mrs. Elliott?"

"Not really." The puzzle still lacked pieces to complete the picture. "Why have you never gone public with this story?"

"Like I said, I had no proof. I also wanted to protect my daughter. As you've already surmised, growing up with my ex-wife for a mother was beyond difficult for Marcella. She's had to deal with enough. I never wanted her hounded by paparazzi and the tabloids."

"That's why she led people to believe she was Lovinia's assistant?"

"One of the few times my daughter has taken my advice. And given the way her mother has treated her, the ruse was easy to pull off."

"Why would she want to work for Lovinia under such circumstances?"

Penelope heaved a huge sigh. "Why does any abuse victim stay with her abuser? Believe me, I tried for years to get her to leave."

"What guarantee do you have that I won't go public with this information?"

"I don't, but you have even less proof than I have."

"Why have you told me all of this?"

He shrugged again. "I woke up this morning and realized I needed to unburden myself to someone after all these years. The truth has weighed heavily on me. You seemed like the logical person, given that you already learned part of the story last night."

"You took a huge risk. I'm not a therapist, a lawyer, or a member of the clergy, which means I'm not bound by any professional rules of confidentiality."

He nodded. "I'm aware of that. However, I believe you're an honorable person."

True, I've never broken the law or cheated on my taxes, and even though I'd betrayed a secret, I'd done so unwittingly. Neither Penelope nor Marcella had requested I keep in confidence what I'd learned at the memorial chapel last night, but I should have known better.

Penelope McIntosh might think I'm an honorable person, but I wasn't feeling all that honorable this morning. I regretted that lapse of judgment. All I could do at this point was hope neither Paisley nor Hyacinth blabbed about the relationship between Penelope, Marcella, and Lovinia.

So no, Penelope McIntosh was wrong. He didn't know anything about me. Or perhaps he knew more than he let on. Paisley had mentioned that many SARA members suspected he held a high-level government job of some sort, and that's why no one knew his real name. Did Penelope McIntosh work for the NSA? Had he compiled a thick dossier on me? Was that even legal?

Don't be ridiculous, Gracie! If the man had that kind of power, he would have been able to find out what really happened the night of the office Christmas party all those years ago. Although, perhaps he did know and had remained silent to keep the mother of his child out of jail.

Maybe Penelope McIntosh has been burdened by a guilty conscience for all these years. By keeping quiet to protect Marcella, he'd inadvertently become complicit in Lovinia's treatment of other authors, not to mention the way she treated her own daughter. Marcella would have been better off had her mother gone to prison, leaving Penelope to raise her.

All sorts of scenarios spun around in my head. The truth might lie hidden somewhere within one of them. Or not. Still, nothing explained why Penelope McIntosh had chosen me as his confessor.

When I didn't challenge his assessment of my character, he added, "If I were wrong about you, the information you learned last night would already be trending on Facebook and Twitter this morning."

I fought to maintain a passive expression, but a lead cannonball had formed in my throat and dropped with a thud into the pit of my tummy. I quickly grabbed my glass of ice water and chugged several huge gulps to stave off the flush threatened to race up my neck and spread throughout my face.

Frankly, I was surprised the news hadn't hit social media yet, but I doubted the silence would last long, thanks to Paisley blabbing to Hyacinth.

At this point all I could say to Penelope was, "I promise not to divulge any of what you've told me this morning." After all, he'd presented me with nothing but wild speculation and conjecture, pure conspiracy theory. Lacking concrete facts, this was a case of he said/she said between a father and his daughter.

I then decided to steer the conversation away from me and back to him and something about him I found odd. "You always refer to Lovinia as your ex-wife or Marcella's mother, never by her real name or even her pen name."

"That's correct."

"Why?"

"I don't care for the pen name she chose. I find it pretentious."

"And her real name?"

"Out of respect for my daughter's wishes, even if I don't agree with her."

Marcella *Ford*. But was "Ford" Lovinia's maiden name, her married name, the surname she adopted, or none of the above? Perhaps "Ford" was Penelope's real given name or his middle name.

One thing I knew for certain: Penelope McIntosh wasn't going to provide me with all the puzzle pieces to solve the mystery of Lovinia Darling. Some he kept locked up inside him; others, even he might not know. However, he'd explained quite a bit to me, and in return I could repay him with some information of my own. However, I had no idea how he'd take the news. "Lovinia's death may not have been an accident."

Penelope's eyebrows shot upward. "What makes you say that?"

I told him what I'd learned this morning. "The woman who filed the lawsuit against Lovinia is staying at the hotel across the street. She may have slipped into the dining room Friday night to watch Lovinia served with the papers and after seeing her rip up the subpoena, confronted her."

"And pushed her down the stairs?"

I nodded. "That's the theory. The police are questioning her."

Penelope leaned back in his chair and stroked the stubble on his chin. "Interesting. I hope it's not true. Lovinia has ruined enough lives. I'd hate to see this woman go to prison over a rash decision made in the heat of the moment, especially since now that my ex-wife is dead, Marcella will quickly and quietly settle the lawsuit out of court."

His reaction struck me as exceedingly calm. Too calm. No

matter how Penelope McIntosh felt about his ex-wife, I would have expected a more emotional response upon learning someone might have murdered her. Unless....

FIFTEEN

I stared at the man sitting across the table from me. Could he have pushed Lovinia down those stairs?

Highly unlikely. If Lovinia and her killer had been arguing in the hallway, someone would have heard them. The killer had to have sneaked up behind Lovinia and shoved her through the door into the stairwell. No way could Penelope sneak up behind anyone, not with his cane-aided lumbering gait. Besides, the man barely had the strength to breathe, let alone walk. If he had heaved the zaftig Lovinia with enough force to send her tumbling down the stairs, he'd most likely have dropped dead from the exertion.

Besides, if Penelope harbored enough resentment toward Lovinia to kill her, why would he have waited so long? No, in my extremely unscientific and decidedly amateur sleuthing opinion, Penelope McIntosh had not murdered his ex-wife.

We sat silently for a few minutes. I sipped at the dregs of my now cold coffee, pondering what I'd just learned, while Penelope concentrated on making certain not a single infinitesimal scrap of egg, bacon, potato, or toast remained on his plate. Once he'd consumed the last vestiges of his breakfast, he signaled the waiter for the check.

"Will you be attending my workshop this morning?" he asked as he wiped his mouth with his napkin.

According to the conference schedule, Penelope was giving a nine o'clock talk on Historically Accurate Historicals. I had little interest in Scottish historical romances—or any historical romance from medieval times, for that matter. If people back then bathed once a year, it was a lot. No matter how much I tried, I couldn't imagine a romantic relationship between a hero and a heroine who reeked to high heaven. I'm too much of a germaphobe. Besides, the thought of all that body odor triggered my gag reflexes.

However, I felt I owed it to Penelope to attend. Adjusting my best fake smile, I said, "Wouldn't dream of missing it."

Together we headed upstairs to the conference room.

The other SARA workshops I'd attended had been standing-room-only with authors filling all the seats and just about every available inch of floor space. Not this morning. As the wall-mounted clock signaled the hour and the moderator began her introduction of Penelope, I glanced around the half-empty room.

Where was everyone? Sleeping in after partying to the wee hours of last night? Attending the other workshops going on at the same time? Or had many authors already departed to catch early morning flights home?

A sense of déjà vu engulfed me. I once gave an interactive trade show workshop that some clueless organizer had scheduled during an NFL playoff game. Six people attended. I had spent days preparing handouts and other materials for a hundred attendees.

I hoped the lack of attendance wasn't due to the speaker. I knew nothing of Penelope McIntosh, the author, other than that his career had spanned decades. I'd never read one of his books. I hoped the lack of bottoms planted in chairs wasn't indicative of the quality of his presentations. Not all writers are great speakers. The two don't always go hand-in-hand. If Penelope didn't know how to captivate an audience, I had a long, boring forty-five minutes ahead of me.

However, the lack of audience didn't appear to faze him. He launched into his talk as if the room were filled to capacity. Forty-five minutes later he finished to a rousing round of applause. Even I—much to my surprise—had enjoyed his presentation. Plus, I learned enough about Scottish castles to want to dart across the pond for a visit. Too bad the needle on my bank account hovered near empty.

After attending one final workshop, I made my way to the ballroom for the closing brunch, scheduled early enough for everyone to meet the one o'clock hotel checkout time. As I stood in line at the buffet table, I scanned the room in search of Paisley and Hyacinth. Finding neither of them, I filled my plate with a selection of salad items, then found a seat at a half-empty table, placing myself facing the main entrance in case either Paisley or Hyacinth arrived.

Neither ever showed. Or if they did, I somehow missed them.

I had expected some sort of farewell speech from the SARA president or conference chair, but no one stepped up to the podium while we ate, and people began filing out of the room once they'd finished their meal. So I did the same, heading upstairs to pack.

I never found Paisley or Hyacinth before Blake and I checked out of the hotel. Before leaving, I picked up the house phone in the lobby, asking to be connected to their shared room, only to find that both had already checked out of the hotel.

A twang of hurt settled inside me. If Paisley and Hyacinth had planned to leave the hotel prior to the brunch and hadn't expected to see me again, why had they not mentioned it at breakfast? Why not say good-bye before heading off to their committee meeting? I certainly hadn't pegged either of them as lacking graciousness, especially after all they'd done for me throughout the weekend.

As Blake and I stood on the cab line in front of the hotel, I sent Paisley a text: Sorry we didn't get a chance to say good-bye. Talk to you soon. Excited about our project.

A few minutes later she replied with a "me 2" and a frowning emoji.

~*~

Writing is hard work. I knew that. However, I hadn't expected writing out of my comfort zone to prove nearly impossible.

"How long are you going to sit there staring at a blinking cursor on a blank page?" asked Blake, coming up behind me as I sat in our shared office.

"Until I figure out a plot or die trying?" I'd returned from the SARA conference eager to begin the book Paisley and I planned to write together, but now three weeks into the project I'd accomplished exactly zilch. No brief summary. No synopsis. No chapters. Not even a single paragraph worth sharing with her.

"What's the problem?" asked Blake.

"In a word? Me."

He placed his hands on my shoulders and gently massaged them. "Care to be more specific?"

"My confidence and my muse have run off together and left no forwarding address."

Blake chuckled.

I whipped my head around to face him. "What's so funny?"

"You." He dipped his head and planted a peck of a kiss on the tip of my nose. "Even when you're upset, you find humor in the situation."

I returned my gaze to my blank computer screen, frowned at the taunting cursor, and huffed out my exasperation. "That's the problem. I'm supposed to be writing a romantic suspense. I need intrigue and angst, not humor."

Blake pulled his desk chair over next to mine and sat beside me. He reached for my hand and held it in both of his. "Gracie, I feel the need to remind you that you don't like to read thrillers or suspense. They creep you out. You won't even watch a James Bond movie."

I shifted in my chair to face him. "Tell me something I don't know." Even though ultimately the hero and heroine prevail in a romantic suspense and the book ends with a happily-ever-after, too many nightmare-inducing scenarios take place between the once-upon-a-time of the first page and when the hero and heroine walk off hand-in-hand into the sunset on the last page.

Plots with suspense and thriller elements always leave me looking over my shoulder and jumping at every unexpected sound for weeks afterwards. That's why I don't read them.

"Serial killers and terrorists are not your idea of entertainment," Blake reminded me.

"That's because real life is scary enough these days. I want to escape what's going on in the world, not constantly be bombarded with reminders of the horrors taking place all over the globe, not to mention right here in our own country."

"Then why are you trying to write a romantic suspense?"

Duh! "Do I really need to state the obvious? Because writing a book in partnership with Paisley Prentiss could make my career. How can I *not* take advantage of her offer?"

"Didn't you tell me Paisley writes romantic comedy?"

I nodded. "*New York Times* bestselling romantic comedy author many times over."

"Has she ever written a romantic suspense?"

I shook my head. "This will be her first."

Blake leaned back in his chair and crossed his arms over his chest. "So let me get this straight: a bestselling author of romantic comedy has offered to team up with an unpublished author of romantic comedy to write a book in a genre neither of you has ever written in and which at least one of you doesn't even read?"

I nodded again.

Blake executed an eye roll. "Why?"

"Uhm..." I worried my lower lip, the answer to his question escaping me.

"What am I missing here, Gracie? Because right now this makes absolutely no sense to me."

"Paisley said she's paying it forward, that when she first started writing, another author helped her and all she asked in return was that if Paisley ever had the chance, she'd do the same for some other writer."

"Fair enough. But why aren't you collaborating on a romantic comedy? Wouldn't that make more sense?"

I couldn't argue with Blake's logic. "Blame it on Lovinia," I said. "So many people hated her. We got carried away speculating that one of them had killed her." And as it turned out, one of them may have done exactly that.

"So you started nosing around, hoping it was true, even though the detective told you her death was an accident? All in the name of figuring out a plot for a book?"

"He never said he was absolutely, positively, one hundred percent certain Lovinia's death was an accident."

Blake speared me with *The Look*.

"Well, he didn't! Besides, that was before Paisley and Hyacinth learned that the woman who filed the plagiarism lawsuit against Lovinia was booked in the hotel across the street from the conference."

The Look persisted.

"She was! The police picked her up for questioning."

"You never mentioned that."

"Didn't I? Are you sure?"

"Trust me. I would have remembered."

Blake had me on the hot seat. All I could say in my defense was, "I guess I forgot?" In reality, I hadn't forgotten. I'd decided nothing good would come of telling Blake about Ronelle Crenshaw until I knew for certain she had killed Lovinia. So I accidentally on purpose allowed the information to slip my mind.

"So what happened?"

I shrugged. "I don't know." Even though I'd continually scoured the news and social media the last three weeks, I'd seen no mention of Ronelle Crenshaw's arrest and not even the slightest media rumor or speculation suggesting someone had killed Lovinia.

"Whether Lovinia was killed or not, Paisley thought someone killing the Queen of Romance over plagiarism would make for a great romantic suspense plot," I continued. "She said she'd been toying with the idea of writing romantic suspense for some time, so why not give it a try? She loved my manuscript, and this was the perfect opportunity for her to keep her promise to 'pay it forward'."

Blake mulled that over for minute before asking, "Who's your hero?"

I sighed. "That's part of my problem. I have a victim, a killer, and a heroine, but I don't have a hero."

"Because you're trying to force a square peg plot into a round hole genre."

I sighed again. Blake had articulated the conclusion I'd already come to on my own, which explained why I continued my unsatisfactory relationship with the blinking cursor and blank page. "Any suggestions?"

"Have you spoken to your co-conspirator?"

"Co-*author*."

"Really? Sounds to me like you're doing all the work. What has Paisley contributed so far?"

"She's on deadline. Once she turns in her latest book, we'll begin working together."

"Then I suggest you stop beating yourself up and wait until she's ready to sit down to work with you on this project—after you have a signed contract."

"I've already spoken to her about a contract, which by the way, her agent also suggested. It's Item Number One on our to-do list."

"I'm happy to hear that."

"Thought you might be," I said, attempting to mimic *The Look*. However, I suspect I failed miserably.

Blake confirmed my suspicion when he roared with laughter. I responded by sticking out my tongue, which unleashed his inner Frenchman. Who could resist? Not me. After all these years the guy still releases tummy butterflies in me, and now was no different.

When we finally separated, I said, "Just so we're clear, that wasn't an invitation."

He winked. "Could have fooled me."

~*~

With Blake's help I'd come to the conclusion I was approaching the writing of a romantic suspense from the wrong direction. If I developed a credible hero, perhaps both my muse and my confidence would return.

I also thought a change of venue might help—for me, not my story. So after Blake headed off to campus, I poured myself a tall glass of mint iced tea, grabbed a pad and pencil, and settled into the cushions of a comfy wicker chair in the screened-in porch situated behind our kitchen. As a gentle cross-breeze wafted around me, I sipped my tea, closed my eyes, and conjured up images of my favorite romance heroes.

Not surprisingly, Luke Bennett, the hero of my now award-winning manuscript, immediately came to mind. But so did the heroes of some of my favorite authors, like Liz Phillips and Elise Robertson, and of course, Paisley Prentiss. I knew exactly the type of hero I wanted to create; I just didn't know how to make him an integral part of a romantic suspense story that takes place at a romance conference.

Few men had attended the SARA conference, mostly because few men write romance. I jotted down a list of categories that included authors, industry professionals, and cover models. Drumming the eraser end of my pencil against the notepad, I thought of the one man I'd gotten to know at the conference— Penelope McIntyre—not exactly hero material, but that hardly mattered. Paisley and I were writing fiction, not true crime. If I chose to cast my hero as the ex-husband of the victim, he might wear jeans and a cowboy hat (romance readers love their cowboys!) but that's where the similarity would end.

Aside from hotel staff, the only other men I'd come in contact with throughout the weekend conference were my own husband and Detective Vanwhatshisname. A romance involving a husband and wife struck me as too unconventional for the genre. Readers want to travel along with the hero and heroine as their emotional and physical relationship develops, rooting for them when conflicts threaten to derail their journey toward happily-ever-after. The sub-genre—contemporary, historical, paranormal, or romantic suspense—didn't matter.

Unless the couple had separated or divorced and the author is writing a reconciliation story, a married couple had already completed their relationship journey. Perhaps a well-established romantic suspense author could get away with a married hero and heroine, but to me, a husband and wife team seemed better suited for a cozy or amateur sleuth mystery series rather than a stand-alone romantic suspense. Besides, why write a book that would give an editor doubts about its salability?

Scratch Blake or any other husband as potential hero material for this book. That left me with a fellow author, a cover model, someone who worked for a publishing house, or the detective investigating the crime. I mulled over my choices, absent-mindedly doodling on my notepad until I happened to glance down at my scribbling. Circles, stars, arrows, and curlicues surrounded one category. My subconscious had zeroed in on the ideal choice—the detective. This made perfect sense, given that, even though I didn't read them, I knew many romantic suspense novels involved a law enforcement professional as the hero. Hopefully, Paisley would agree.

I grabbed my cell phone and sent her a quick text: How about detective as hero?

She responded immediately with a thumbs-up emoji.

I texted back: How's the ms. going?

Her reply? A thumbs-down emoji.

Me: When do you think you'll finish?

Her: a shrugging emoji.

I realized Paisley's contractual work came before a spec manuscript. An author's first responsibility is to meet her deadlines, but I couldn't help but feel more than a teensy bit disappointed. I also hadn't heard from either Paisley's agent or her editor yet.

My practical side told me I might wait months to hear anything about my manuscript, but patience was never one of my virtues. I wanted to ask Paisley if she'd heard anything from either woman but realized asking was pointless. If she knew something, she'd tell me.

So I sucked up my disappointment and plowed ahead, sketching out ideas now that I'd settled on a hero for our story. At least I was no longer staring at a blinking cursor on a blank screen. Progress was progress, even when measured in baby steps, right?

However, the more I thought about my fictional detective, whom I'd decided to name Cooper Landon, the more my thoughts wandered away from my manuscript. Instead, my brain kept traveling back to Detective Vanwhatshisname and the lack of news regarding Lovinia's death. The detective had given me his card and told me to call him if I remembered anything. I didn't, but my curiosity needed satisfying.

I headed upstairs and searched through the piles of papers I'd accumulated from the conference until I found the small white card. Before placing the call, I practiced pronouncing his name out loud until my tongue stopped tripping over the syllables. Once satisfied I wouldn't butcher it, I grabbed my phone and keyed in the numbers.

He answered on the second ring. "Vanslootenberger."

Relieved that I didn't have to ask for him, I said, "Hello, Detective. This is Gracie Elliott."

"Who?"

Was I that forgettable? Here I was hoping to become a bestselling author, and the guy who spent hours questioning me about a death three weeks ago didn't even remember me? Vanwhatshisname had just pulverized my already crushed ego into dust. "From the writers conference? The one who found Lovinia Darling's body?"

"I know who you are, Mrs. Elliott. I was yanking your chain. What can I do for you?"

Someone definitely needs to work on his sense of humor, but I prudently kept that thought to myself. "I was wondering about the status of the case."

"The case?"

"I heard you picked up Ronelle Crenshaw for questioning."

Silence followed. Vanwhatshisname said nothing for so long that I thought the call had been disconnected or worse yet, that he'd hung up on me. "Detective?"

Finally he cleared his throat and in a clipped tone said, "I'm afraid I'm not at liberty to discuss an ongoing investigation, Mrs. Elliott." And then he did hang up.

I stared totally dumbfounded at the phone in my hand. Over

the past year I'd come in contact with several law enforcement officers and drawn the conclusion that the police academy curriculum lacked any courses in the social graces.

Granted, given the state of the country and the world, other disciplines were far more important than studying Emily Post. Catching criminals far outweighed satisfying the curiosity of a budding author, even if that budding author had discovered a dead body. Still, the guy really should work on his people skills.

Meanwhile, I decided I needed to set my writing aside and concentrate on restocking our depleted fridge. I hate going to the supermarket and tend to put it off until we're down to a dinner choice between take-out or a meal of dry cornflakes. Since Blake and I had gone to our favorite local Chinese restaurant last night, and we were also out of cornflakes, I girded my loins for a trip to the supermarket.

Forty-five minutes later I was pulling the last bag of groceries from the trunk of my car when a black sedan pulled into my driveway. Detective Vanwhatshisname opened the driver's side door, stepped from behind the wheel, and asked, "Who the hell is Ronelle Crenshaw?"

The grocery bag slipped from my arms, spilling its contents across my driveway.

SIXTEEN

An hour later I parked my car at the curb across the street from Paisley's house in Short Hills, New Jersey, a town where the average income qualifies most of its residents as one-percenters. Not only will a small home in Short Hills set a buyer back more than a million dollars, annual property taxes exceed the yearly salaries of many Americans. However, there are few small homes in Short Hills, and from my vantage point Paisley Prentiss certainly didn't live in one. I whistled under my breath as I took in the sprawling, corner lot Tudor manse, easily three times the size of my own home.

Paisley had never told me where she lived. I had mistakenly assumed she'd flown to New York for the conference. Given that many authors worry about unhinged fans stalking them, I wondered if Paisley realized how easily someone could find her. I'd uncovered her address in less than ten minutes and was relieved to find she lived a short car ride away. The conversation I intended to have with her demanded a face-to-face meeting. Paisley had lied to me, and I wanted to know why.

I unbuckled my seatbelt, stepped from my Camry, and marched across the street to confront her. The house, traditionally painted in cream and brown and sparkling in the dappled early June sunlight, looked like it was posing for a spread in *Home and Garden*, which was actually what had aided me in pinpointing its location. Last year the magazine had done a series on the homes of romance authors. The article not only mentioned the town, the photo had captured part of the corner street sign and the house number prominently displayed in the leaded glass window above her front door.

As I traversed the cobblestone walkway that led to the main entrance, I scoped out the perfectly manicured grounds, envisioning a team of gardeners clipping each blade of grass by hand. Other authors might be feeling the pinch in today's publishing world, but Paisley Prentiss wasn't one of them. Publishers Marketplace had listed her latest advance as a "major deal," which placed it at half a million dollars or more. I had no idea what Mr. Prentiss did for a living, but I suspected he earned quite a bit more than my own husband's college professor salary.

I climbed the two steps to the front door and rang the doorbell. Seconds slipped by as I waited, but given the size of the house, I didn't expect the door to swing open immediately. When it finally did, Paisley took one look at me, gasped, and said, "What are you doing here?"

"Hello to you, too, Paisley."

"Gracie, I'm really bogged down. I wish you had called. Today is not a good day. I don't have time to socialize."

"I'm not here to socialize." I pushed open the door and stepped into her foyer before she had a chance to close the door on me—

something I suspected had crossed her mind, given the expression on her face.

"Why are you here?" she asked.

"I want to know why you lied to me."

"Why would you think I lied to you?"

"Because I know Ronelle Crenshaw was never questioned by the police."

Her hand gripped the edge of the door so tightly I could see her knuckles turning white. The ghostly color matched her face. "Well, maybe Detective Vanslootenberger discovered she had an alibi for the time of Lovinia's death, so he didn't have to question her."

How the heck did she remember his name when I never could? "You never called the detective."

"No, uhm...Hyacinth placed the call."

I shook my head. "Give it up, Paisley. No one called him because Ronelle was never in New York during the conference. Neither you nor Hyacinth ever spoke with Ronelle's husband."

"How do you know that?"

"We'll discuss that later." I grabbed the door out of her hand and closed it behind us, planting myself between her and the closed door, my legs spread, my hands on my hips. "For now I want to know what kind of game the two of you were playing at my expense and why."

Paisley's shoulders sagged. "Will you promise not to breathe a word to anyone?"

I nodded. "I just want the truth."

She sighed. "Let's sit down."

I followed her into the living room, the furnishings familiar to me from the *Home and Garden* spread, and took a seat at one end of the gray microfiber sectional sofa. Paisley remained standing, pacing back and forth in front of the stacked stone fireplace. "I'm not sure where to start," she said, her voice catching.

Was she trying to play on my sympathies? I was the wronged party here. I stared stonily at her and said, "Try at the beginning."

"It's not that simple."

"Deceit rarely is."

She cast pleading eyes at me. "I didn't mean for any of this to happen, Gracie. You wound up in the wrong place at the wrong time, and I needed to protect myself."

"From me?"

"From what you may have seen or heard."

"About what?"

She inhaled a deep breath, released it quickly, then whispered, "About Lovinia's death."

I gasped. "Did you kill Lovinia, Paisley?"

She clenched her fists and squeezed her eyes shut. "I didn't mean to. It was an accident. You have to believe me."

"Why?"

"Because I'm telling you the truth."

"No, why did you kill her?"

Paisley collapsed into a gray and white chevron print chair flanking the fireplace. She lowered her head into her hands and sobbed. I waited patiently while she cried for a few minutes, but my patience grew thin as the mantle clock ticked away the seconds. "Paisley?"

She lifted her head and sucked in air. "Because she killed my mother."

The missing puzzle piece fell into place. I knew the answer to the question I was about to ask, but Paisley didn't know I knew.

"How?"

She swiped at her tears with both hands. Do you remember how I mentioned my father had recently died?"

I nodded. "You were going through all his belongings and stumbled upon journals he'd kept."

She nodded. "I was only four years old when my mother died. I really don't remember her."

"How was Lovinia responsible for her death?"

"I grew up believing my mother died from an aortic aneurysm. It wasn't until I read my father's journals that I discovered the truth. He was convinced my mother died from a cocaine overdose—cocaine that Lovinia gave her. Only she wasn't Lovinia back then. She was Yvette Sokalov. My mother worked for her."

I played dumb. "Why didn't your father go to the police?"

"Because he had no proof." She began to tell me much the same story I'd heard from Penelope. "After my mother's death, Yvette left her job and changed both her name and her looks. My father detailed how he bumped into her one day about a year after my mother died.

"He was standing in line at the bank and noticed this extremely tall woman in the line next to him. Something about her seemed familiar. As soon as he heard her speak to the teller he knew she was Yvette. He immediately recognized her voice."

"After a year? How often had he come in contact with her while your mother was alive?"

"Not often in person but apparently she had a habit of calling my mother at home in the evenings and on weekends. Dad often answered the phone. He wrote that she treated Mom more like a servant who should be available twenty-four/seven, rather than a nine-to-five employee."

That certainly sounded like Lovinia from what I'd overheard from the publishing professionals at the conference luncheon. "Did he confront her?"

Paisley nodded. "Of course, she denied being Yvette."

"So she never admitted to him that she'd given your mother cocaine?"

"No."

"What about an autopsy?" Penelope had claimed one was never performed.

"According to what Dad wrote, preliminary tests confirmed the aneurism. The doctor never looked beyond that."

Again, confirming Penelope's hypothesis about the doctor. Or maybe not. Paisley's mother may never have snorted cocaine at the office Christmas party. Her father needed someone to blame for the loss of his wife. The cocaine snorting Lovinia was the perfect target. "What happened after that?"

"He hired a private investigator who discovered Yvette had transformed into Lovinia. It's all in his journals."

"And he never said a word to you, not even after you became a successful author in the same genre?"

"Never." She lowered her head and ran shaky fingers through her pixie cut. "He probably planned to destroy the journals at some point, or maybe he forgot about them. His memory began failing toward the end of his life." She lifted her head and focused on me. "Dementia. I doubt he ever intended for me to find the journals and read them."

"You said you didn't mean to kill Lovinia. What happened?"

"After you decided to walk up to your room, I caught an elevator. Lovinia was in the car. I had only read the journals two days earlier. I wanted to confront her at the conference, and this was my opportunity. When she got off the elevator at her floor, I followed her."

"Did you push her down the stairs?"

"Not deliberately. When I approached her and told her who I was and that I knew she was responsible for my mother's death, she laughed at me. She said no one twisted my mother's arm and forced her to snort cocaine. That's when I lost it and pushed her. She fell through the door. You know the rest."

Had Lovinia actually witnessed Paisley's mother using coke? Or did Lovinia and her white powder play no role in the woman's death? The truth of that night had died first with Paisley's mother, then with Lovinia. "I don't understand why you didn't call the police."

"I panicked."

"You left her to die. You're no better than she was."

"How dare you! She killed my mother."

"And you killed her. Where's the difference, Paisley?"

She glared at me. "My mother didn't deserve to die."

"Why draw me into all of this?"

"I needed to make certain you hadn't seen or heard me."

"So you concocted this elaborate ruse to cover your tracks?"

She hung her head. "I'm sorry, Gracie. You have to believe me. I didn't know what else to do."

"Did you ever intend to write a book with me?"

She shook her still lowered head. "I meant what I said about paying it forward, though. That's why I introduced you to my agent and editor."

"You never read my manuscript and sent it to your editor, did you?"

Another shake of her head. "No."

"And Hyacinth was in on all this?"

"She's my best friend."

"You didn't answer the question."

She nodded. "After we learned you'd already solved one murder, she helped me keep misdirecting you."

Paisley's doorbell rang. She rose to answer it. I followed her. She opened the door, and a familiar voice said, "Paisley Prentiss, you're under arrest for the murder of Lovinia Darling."

Paisley spun around to confront me. "You set me up?"

Without saying anything, I unbuttoned the top two buttons of my shirt to expose the wire I wore.

As two uniformed officers led Paisley to a waiting squad car, she twisted her neck to throw a parting shot at me from over her shoulder, "I hope you're happy, Gracie. You've destroyed any chance of ever getting published. No editor or agent will want to work with you. I'll see to that."

~*~

Detective Vanwhatshisname and I stood on the sidewalk outside Paisley's palatial Tudor and watched the squad car pull away from the curb. As it drove off down the street, the detective, now in possession of the wire, turned to me and said, "You did good, Mrs. Elliott." He extended his hand toward me. "I'm proud to know you. Thank you for your help."

Although I shook his hand as I nodded, I felt conflicted. Yes, I'd helped the police solve a murder—one they hadn't even realized needed solving because they hadn't suspected murder played a role in Lovinia's death. However, I also found myself in the throes of one of those there-but-for-the-grace-of-god-go-I moments. Had I discovered decades after the fact that Lovinia caused my mother's death, I could be the one on my way to lockup.

I didn't blame Paisley for what she did in the heat of the moment; I felt sorry for her.

On the other hand, I couldn't forgive her for manipulating me in a misguided scheme to protect herself. Ironically, had she not drawn me into such a convoluted web of lies, no one would ever have known she killed Lovinia. The police would have written off the death of the Queen of Romance as a tragic accident. Paisley's lies were her downfall.

I'd like to think that had I inadvertently killed Lovinia, I would have owned up to it. Of course, I then would have thrown myself on the mercy of the court, hoping a jury of my peers would take pity on me. "What's going to happen to her?" I asked.

He glanced over his shoulder at the huge house and shrugged. "She'll probably hire the best lawyers money can buy and get off with a sentence of a few months at most. My guess is she won't serve a day, but you never know how a jury will react."

"Does that bother you? That she might get away with murder?"

"Manslaughter. I doubt the D.A. will bring murder charges. He'd have to prove premeditation."

"Manslaughter, then."

He stood with his hands in his pockets, his lips pursed. Finally, he said, "Some cases bother me more than others."

His cryptic answer gave no clue as to where this particular case fell for him. Perhaps he, too, found himself conflicted, given that Paisley wasn't a cold-blooded killer, just a cold-blooded liar who lost her temper and made a huge mistake.

After thanking me one last time, he headed down the block to where he'd parked his car.

After he drove off I sat behind the wheel of my Camry, caught in the aftermath of the adrenaline rush that had carried me through the last couple of hours. My hands shook; tears swam in my eyes and spilled down my cheeks. My emotions roller-coastered from hurt to anger and back again. Part of me blamed Paisley and Hyacinth for how they had used me, but the other part of me blamed myself for being so desperate to become a published author that I allowed myself to fall for their machinations. Gullible Gracie.

Eventually, I pulled myself together and drove home. Blake had already returned from campus. I found him in the kitchen putting away the non-perishable groceries I'd deposited on the kitchen counter earlier. Employing a mash-up of fifties sitcom icons, he said, "Gracie, you have some 'splainin to do."

Boy, did I ever! But Blake couldn't possibly know where I'd been or what I'd done while he was meeting with his department chair. Or could he? And if so, how did he find out? "What do you mean?"

"Why were there broken eggshells and dried raw egg all over the driveway?"

"Oh that!" After I dropped the bag of groceries, Detective Vanwhatsisname had helped me retrieve the contents, but the eggs were a total loss. I figured I'd clean up the mess after he left, never expecting to leave with him. But that's exactly what had happened after our conversation and a quick Internet search to find Paisley's address. I totally forgot about the eggs, especially since all evidence of them had disappeared by the time I arrived home.

Blake nailed me with *The Look*. "What did you think I meant?" He paused for a moment, then added, "Where have you been?"

Yup, I had some 'splainin to do. I grabbed two wine glasses, then opened the fridge and pulled out a bottle of Sauvignon blanc. "Have a seat, Blake. This 'splainin is going to take some wine and some time."

I drained half the contents of my glass before finding the courage to begin, but once I started, the words poured out of me. After I'd finished, I took a deep breath before adding, "So as it turns out, you were right all along. I was blinded by ambition, so desperate to get published that I didn't realize Paisley's friendship and her offer to collaborate on a book were too good to be true."

And now I'd probably never get published if Paisley had any say in the matter. If nothing else, neither her agent nor her editor would want to work with me. In obtaining Paisley's confession, I'd destroyed their cash cow. Paisley might not do much prison time, if any, but she'd be tied up with defense attorneys for the foreseeable future. No way she'd meet her deadline now, and if she did go to prison, it might be years before she wrote another book—if ever. I doubted being known as the killer of the Queen of Romance would be good for her career.

Blake sat silently for a minute, sipping at his wine and studying me over the rim of his glass. Finally, he said, "Maybe you shouldn't be kicking yourself, Gracie."

"What do you mean?"

"If you *hadn't* believed Paisley, she would have gotten away with murder."

Good point. Leave it to my husband to find the one thing to say to put everything into perspective. What would I do without him? Still, the devil in me decided to have a bit of fun at Blake's expense. I sighed. "I guess I'm two for two when it comes to solving murders. Maybe I should consider going for a P.I. license."

As expected, he shot me *The Look*.

I responded by reaching for his hand. *Me a P.I.? Really?*

"Gracie...?"

"Or not." I winked and led him toward our bedroom.

A NOTE FROM THE AUTHOR

Dear Reader,

I hope you enjoyed *Literally Dead*, the second book in my Empty Nest Mystery series. If so, please consider leaving a review at your favorite review site.

Gracie really did write a romantic comedy called *Hooking Mr. Right*. (Well, actually I did under my Emma Carlyle pen name.) If you're a mystery reader who also enjoys reading romantic comedy, buy links for *Hooking Mr. Right* can be found on my website at www.loiswinston.com.

Happy reading!
Lois Winston

ABOUT THE AUTHOR

USA Today and Amazon bestselling and award-winning author Lois Winston writes mystery, romance, romantic suspense, chick lit, women's fiction, children's chapter books, and nonfiction under her own name and her Emma Carlyle pen name. *Kirkus Reviews* dubbed her critically acclaimed Anastasia Pollack Crafting Mystery series, "North Jersey's more mature answer to Stephanie Plum." In addition, Lois is an award-winning craft and needlework designer who often draws much of her source material for both her characters and plots from her experiences in the crafts industry. Learn more about Lois and her books, where to find her on social media, and a link for signing up for her newsletter at www.loiswinston.com.

Made in the USA
Monee, IL
08 December 2022

20033151R00132